D. P

W9-DFR-158

Viking Lio...
915 Fir Avenue West
...ns Falls MN 56537
218 9...

"Don't believe everything you hear."

Julia bit her lip. She shouldn't have let her fury take hold of her tongue. Now she would have to apologize, which was the last thing she wanted to do when she was still so mad. They pulled up before the clubhouse. The place reeked of money, just like Robbie. She needed to guard her heart and her tongue better. There was no sense fighting with him. She shouldn't know him well enough to fight.

Robert hopped out of the car and carefully closed the door behind him, then came around and opened her door. He stood stiffly, as if he were a footman and she the mistress.

"Listen, I—"

"You need say no more, Miss Wren." His jaw was so tight it was a wonder he could talk at all. "You may not wish to see it, but the likeliest possibility is that a Townie threw that stone. I intend to find out who it was and see them punished."

Julia's chin climbed a notch. "You're wrong. If anyone, it was a Parkie, and I'll prove it."

LISA KARON RICHARDSON

Influenced by books like *The Little Princess*, Lisa Karon Richardson's early stories were heavy on boarding schools and creepy houses. Now, even though she's (mostly) grown-up, she still loves a healthy dash of adventure in any story she creates, even her own. She's been a missionary to Africa, and now that she and her husband are back in America, they are starting a daughter-work church and raising a family. You can find Lisa at inkwellinspirations.com or at lisakaronrichardson.com.

LISA KARON RICHARDSON

An Unscripted Courtship

HEARTSONG
PRESENTS

If you purchased this book without a cover you should be aware
that this book is stolen property. It was reported as "unsold and
destroyed" to the publisher, and neither the author nor the
publisher has received any payment for this "stripped book."

Recycling programs
for this product may
not exist in your area.

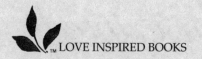

LOVE INSPIRED BOOKS

ISBN-13: 978-0-373-48763-9

An Unscripted Courtship

Copyright © 2015 by Lisa Karon Richardson

All rights reserved. Except for use in any review, the reproduction
or utilization of this work in whole or in part in any form by any
electronic, mechanical or other means, now known or hereinafter
invented, including xerography, photocopying and recording, or in
any information storage or retrieval system, is forbidden without
the written permission of the editorial office, Love Inspired Books,
233 Broadway, New York, NY 10279 U.S.A.

This is a work of fiction. Names, characters, places and incidents are
either the product of the author's imagination or are used fictitiously, and
any resemblance to actual persons, living or dead, business establishments,
events or locales is entirely coincidental.

This edition published by arrangement with Love Inspired Books.

® and TM are trademarks of Love Inspired Books, used under license.
Trademarks indicated with ® are registered in the United States Patent
and Trademark Office, the Canadian Intellectual Property Office and in
other countries.

www.Harlequin.com

Printed in U.S.A.

A good name is rather to be chosen than great
riches, and loving favor rather than silver and gold.
—*Proverbs* 22:1

For Nathan, who reminds me a little bit of Robbie Malcolm.
Love you, Bub!

Chapter 1

We know what we are, but know not what we
may be.

—Shakespeare, Hamlet, Act 4, Scene 5

Tuxedo Park, New York, 1901

Robert Malcolm stopped short and raised his face to
the breeze, imagining himself as a bloodhound scent-
ing prey. He held up a hand to silence his companions.
He thought he'd heard something.

Chattering and laughing, the others failed to notice and plowed into him. He staggered forward, the
bark of a tree biting into his palms as he reached out to
steady himself. He rubbed his hands against his pants
and shook his head.

"Robbie, what is it?" Geraldine Scott demanded, her
voice wavering between pique and concern.

"Shh!" He rubbed his hands against his pants again. He wanted one of his cameras, even his little Kodak Brownie. Without one he always felt out of kilter. It was the way he framed the world. But after that last set-to with his father, they'd all been confiscated. The idea of an adventure, however short-lived it would likely be, felt both liberating and all wrong if he couldn't capture its essence on film.

There it came again, the faint sound of laughter. Ears almost itching from listening so hard, Robert stepped off the dirt path. The foliage welcomed him with the mossy, green smell of unspoiled wilderness. Who could it be? Whoever it was, he meant to make the most of anything unexpected.

"I hear it, too." Charlie Morton pushed his way forward.

Robbie grabbed for his collar. "Hold up there, chum." This was his adventure and he'd be dashed if Charlie was going to take it over. "I'll take the lead."

Assuming the point position, Robbie stepped carefully through the thick, late summer undergrowth. The others trooped behind him as subtle as a marching band. Their smothered giggles grated on his nerves. He ought to have ditched them all and come back on his own.

The trees thinned and grew more windblown. They'd come nearly to the lake's edge. Robbie took refuge behind the last line of trees and stopped.

Along the edge of a tiny cove formed by a natural outcrop of stone, two young people reclined on the grass in bathing costumes. A pretty young woman in a bathing suit stood before them gesturing broadly. Robbie squinted, making sure his eyes weren't deceiving him.

They were villagers. Villagers sporting in Tuxedo Park as if they had a perfect right to the place.

This was better than he'd dared hope.

Standing right at his shoulder, Geraldine gave an outraged snort. "How dare they!"

Robbie held a finger to his lips. "Let's see what they're up to."

She scowled, but held her peace.

Robbie knew the girl declaiming before her friends. It was Julia Wren, the daughter of the owner of the local ice cream parlor. But she was different from the last time he'd seen her. Gone were the pigtails and pinafore. He edged just a hair more around the tree. She was more than pretty—she was beautiful, with luminous eyes of iris blue, dark hair and fair skin. Yet the change in her was more than the fact that she had blossomed into womanhood. She held herself with confidence. Her words held her friends in thrall.

They held him in thrall, too.

Longing again for his camera, he decided to risk getting closer.

Julia bowed at the waist, her loosely braided hair flopping over her shoulder.

"Bravo!" Her friends Minna and Friedrich Bauer jumped to their feet. "Encore!"

"I think it's brilliant, Julia." Minna sprang forward and gave her a hug. "Your professor is going to love it. You will get an A for sure."

Friedrich was more decorous, but he reached for Julia's hand and raised it to his lips. "Delightful, dear Julia." His tawny, close-cropped hair was still damp and darker than usual, but his eyes were the same vivid blue as always.

The intensity in his gaze made her cast her eyes to the ground and she gently withdrew her hand. She opened her mouth to thank him.

"Brilliant indeed." A more languid clapping came from Julia's right. She spun in the direction of the unexpected sound.

Robert Malcolm stepped from the woods flanked by several other Parkies. The leading lights of their set. Her hands grew suddenly clammy. The jig was up. Her friends depended upon their jobs at the Park, and now her desire for a lark had gotten them in big trouble.

She didn't say anything. What could she say? Minna and Friedrich stood shoulder to shoulder with her. In Julia's imagination they were the gallant underdogs, facing a vastly superior force. Lines from "The Charge of the Light Brigade" began spooling through her mind. *Half a league half a league, Half a league onward.*

Mr. Malcolm stopped about six feet from her.

Julia found her voice. "We're leaving."

He raised an eyebrow. "Now why would you want to do that? It seemed as if you were all having such a jolly time."

The response flustered Julia. She had half expected the Parkies to produce horsewhips and drive them from the Park. She sensed a trap, but her pride nudged her. "We were having a jolly time."

Harriet Vines, thin faced and purse-lipped, crossed her arms with the air of someone longing for a horsewhip. She settled for words with nearly as much sting. "Minna, it distresses me to think how disappointed Mama will be when I inform her of this transgression.

We simply can't continue to employ a maid who doesn't know her place and sneaks about like this on her half day."

Julia flinched for her friend. The high flush in Minna's face fled and she dropped her gaze to the ground, but she did not move away from Julia's side. Friedrich stepped forward, his hands curled into tight fists at his sides.

Harriet opened her mouth to say something to him, but to Julia's surprise, Mr. Malcolm gave Harriet a withering look and she subsided. "Tell me about this play you were acting out. Some parody on Shakespeare?"

Warily, Julia appraised him. Why was he so interested?

Now both eyebrows rose.

She forbore from sighing. "It's called *A Tempest in a Teapot*. I reimagined *The Tempest* in a modern American setting. In a place much like Tuxedo Park in fact."

"Sounds droll." The ever-elegant Geraldine Scott said in a voice that meant the opposite as she fluffed the frills on her parasol.

"I don't know. It could be intriguing." Mr. Malcolm settled himself on a rock. "Why *The Tempest?*"

Julia smiled wryly. "Originally? Because I liked Ferdinand and Miranda the best of any of Shakespeare's lovers."

"More so than Romeo and Juliet?" His eyes danced with light. "I thought it was something of a requirement that young ladies fall madly in love with dashing Romeo."

"A silly, ill-considered popinjay," Julia responded promptly.

"And Juliet?"

"Misguided, obtuse and overhasty."

Once again Mr. Malcolm's eyebrows rose and a rogue's smile flashed across his face. "'Though she be but little, she is fierce.'"

Julia bit her lip to keep from responding with a grin of her own. No sense in letting him know she didn't have the upper hand. Which of course, he already did know. But still. No need to reinforce his superior position.

Charlie Morton had followed Mr. Malcolm's lead and claimed a tussock to sit on. Despite the tittering of the other Parkies, he ignored his fellow's jest. "Don't you think that's rather missing the point?"

"Perhaps," Julia said, "but I have little patience for Romeo and Juliet and their ilk." Wondering how on earth they had fallen into an actual conversation, but cautious as if she were placating a pack of guard dogs, Julia smiled without baring her teeth.

Friedrich and Minna began discreetly clearing away the remains of their picnic lunch. Used to servants moving about them unremarked, the Parkies didn't even seem to notice.

Miss Scott's fan swished in irritated cadence as if she couldn't understand why they were still wasting time on Townies. Her gaze settled on Julia. "I suppose you think you can do a better job than the great playwright?"

Trust her to put claws to the conversation. Julia's cheeks grew hot with choking down the retort that sprang to her lips. Geraldine had had this effect on her ever since they were children, when Julia had had to wait on the selfish twit anytime she came into the ice cream parlor.

Friedrich made a strangled sound of protest. "You know nothing of—"

Julia gripped his arm. Then deliberately willed away the tension in her jaw. "This is an assignment for a class at Barnard."

Geraldine smiled at her sweetly. "Oh, yes. I'd heard that you decided you weren't likely to find a husband and were chasing an education instead." The smile ended with a point as sharp as a knife. "It was probably a wise decision."

"As was your decision not to attempt anything so mentally taxing."

Minna glanced at Julia as if she were crazy. Julia breathed deeply. She needed to rein in her temper for their sake, if not her own. Their jobs at the Park were on the line. And she was in the wrong for having enticed them to join her in sneaking into the Park anyway.

She glanced back to Mr. Malcolm and found that he looked more amused than upset, and faintly surprised. "I thought your innovations rather charming, Miss Wren." His eyes were full of mischief and humor when they found hers. "I think it would be the perfect project for our amateur theatrical."

Julia stared at him, feeling as if the bear trap had sprung but so shocked she couldn't quite feel the bite yet. Mr. Malcolm's friends gazed at him with almost as much horror as she felt.

Friedrich, scowling and fierce as an avenging angel, spoke for her. "Why would you want to do that?"

Mr. Malcolm's response was almost languid. "As I said, I found it amusing. It could be interesting to do something unique."

"We had planned on *A Doll's House*." Geraldine's tone was taut.

"That old chestnut has been done to death." Mr. Malcolm stood. "What we need is an amusing new challenge. And the best person to direct it is its author."

The bear trap had fully closed. Julia shook her head. "No. Oh, no. I don't think so. Miss Scott is right. It would be better for you all to put on *A Doll's House*." She glanced to Minna for support. "I mean that's real literature. It's—um—dramatic and challenging and has a lot of substance for you to work with."

"No. We do enough of those. We can stand a break from taking ourselves so seriously. A comedy will be perfect. And I do hope you'll allow us to use your play." He paused for the briefest moment. "Perhaps if we promise not to make an issue of your indiscretion in trespassing on private property?"

His friends' eyes flew to him, and he stared hard at each one in turn until they glanced away.

Julia could almost hear the squeal of metal as the trap ratcheted tighter. "I—that is—" Her throat tightened and she felt so hot that if she jumped into the lake, she'd have set it boiling.

Miss Scott stepped up to Mr. Malcolm's shoulder, her face set in hard planes while his was relaxed, almost neutral. "I would hate for there to be any repercussions for your friends here." Her words were grudging, almost as if they were being dragged from her by force. "It is a tough time to be out of work and without a reference. But if you will comply with Mr. Malcolm's wishes, we will not need to say any more of what we've seen here today."

Julia looked at each of the Parkies in turn, but their

expressions gave little away. Even Miss Vines. Julia couldn't decide whether it was satisfaction at her own distress, or Mr. Malcolm's influence which swayed Miss Scott. Either way, the little blister made no more complaints and no more threats. Anything Julia said now would only make things worse. Wincing at the trap's bite, she handed the script to Mr. Malcolm then reached to shake his hand. They had a bargain. She would have to trust him to keep up his end.

Chapter 2

Julia slammed into her house and stomped upstairs. How dare they? How dare they! The Parkies were so—so insufferable. So supercilious. So smug. She didn't want their judgmental scrutiny aimed at her words.

The bedsprings groaned as she flung herself down. And making her director. That was a cruel twist of the knife. She'd be audience to their disdain throughout the casting, practices and the show. A high price to pay for a swim.

But there was no backing out. The swim had been her idea and she had all but coerced Minna and Friedrich into joining her. She would not have them lose their jobs on account of her poor judgment. There was nothing to do but grin and bear the consequences.

She lay disconsolate until it was time to start dinner. Pop wouldn't be pleased when he heard that she would have to take time away from the ice cream parlor to help put on an amateur theatrical at the Park. It was their busiest season. Come to think of it, she should make a very special dinner. She needed him in the best possible mood before springing the news on him.

Now that she had a plan, she bounded down the stairs and got busy in the kitchen. A nice filet and fresh snap peas with a bowl of strawberries and whipped cream. That would be the ticket. First she set to making some soda bread. It wouldn't require time to rise, but would have a lovely crust and lots of nooks and crannies for the butter to melt into. And it wouldn't hurt any that it was Pop's favorite.

Busy with her tasks, she hummed as she moved and spun around the small kitchen almost as if performing a dance. All of life was a sort of dance. Step and reverse. She could handle it with grace or not as she chose. She grabbed a pencil and a scrap of paper to write that down. It would work perfectly for her heroine's soliloquy in the—

A throat cleared behind her. She squeaked, dropped the pencil and whirled to find Friedrich standing in the doorway, looking like a golden statue brought to life in the late afternoon sun.

"Good heavens." She put a flour-dusted hand over her heart, then swiped at the palm print she'd left. "You scared the daylights out of me."

"Sorry." He held up both hands. "I didn't mean to sneak up on you."

She dug deep and found a smile for him. "Never mind. It's only the second time I've been surprised today, and at least this surprise is more pleasant."

Shaking his head, Friedrich entered the kitchen and

claimed a stool. "That was quite a scene. It makes me mad how they think they can control everyone." He picked up a pea pod and snapped it in two. "Tell us all where we can go and where we can't. As if they are so much better than the rest of us." He popped half in his mouth and chewed.

Julia paused, her hands frozen in mid-task. "I'm so sorry I dragged you and Minna there. It wasn't worth the thrill. That's for sure."

His mouth drew down in a frown. "Do not fret yourself. The whole idea of the Parkies building their enclave on our backs and then allowing us in only so we can serve them. It's…" His disgust was written in the curl of his lip and the chill in his eyes. "I'm glad you were bold enough to suggest it. It's made me think about some things. You're not really going to let them use your play, surely? That Malcolm would love to turn you into some sort of indentured servant for the duration."

With more force than strictly necessary, Julia attacked the task of tenderizing the meat. "I don't have a choice, Friedrich." Thwack.

"Of course you have a choice. There's always a choice." He leaned against the counter beside her, arms crossed over his chest.

"No." Thwack. "There's not always a choice." Thwack. "I have to do this."

"You have to, or you want to? I saw the way Robert Malcolm was looking at you. I think you want to work with the Parkies. You want to impress them, as if their opinions are more valid than mine and Minna's."

Brandishing the meat mallet, Julia wheeled to face him. "The only reason I ever agreed to allow them to use my play was to make sure that you and Minna didn't lose your jobs. I felt a sense of responsibility. The least you could do is thank me."

Friedrich's nostrils flared and two spots of color burned high in his cheeks. "Thank you! Thank you? We didn't ask you to do anything of the kind. Like I said, it was your choice. The Parkies always do this. They take anything that is ours. They see anything of beauty or worth and they appropriate it." His voice grew softer. "I thought that of all people you understood that. Understood that they would try to pillage your talent, your words." Shaking his head, he stalked away, ripped open the screen door and allowed it to smack closed behind him.

Julia watched him go, her fingers tightening on the mallet. How could he behave like that? As if she had betrayed him, when all she was trying to do was protect him. Besides it was all over something so silly. The play wasn't really important. Deliberately she laid aside the mallet and poured out the cream into a bowl. She measured in some sugar and began whipping the mixture. Anyway, it was her play to do with as she wished. What right did he have ordering her about?

Even Robert Malcolm, the biggest playboy in the Park, had asked her, not ordered her. Although his pals did force the issue with thinly veiled threats.

What look had Friedrich noticed? She hadn't seen Robbie for a while, and he had taken her by surprise. The lanky youth of yore was gone, replaced by a man with a hint of leashed energy beneath the suavity of tailored suit and fine manners. And dark eyes—dark, mysterious, challenging, beautiful eyes.

Julia shook herself from her reverie. There was no percentage in that path. She knew exactly what Robbie

Malcolm was, and she had no intention of dashing all her dreams against the rocks of scandal.

Geraldine's chatter sloshed around Robbie much like the waves sloshed about their rowboat, and he paid them about as much attention. His imagination was occupied with conjuring mounded black clouds bristling with lightning and the angry grumble of thunder. The surface of the lake began to shudder with the knowledge of the coming storm. A tempest raged in his mind.

Before him loomed an island, craggy and foreboding. In his mind's eye he could just make out a figure standing on an outcrop, arms raised, the rags of a once fine suit flapping in tatters around him. Prospero.

If he listened hard above the gale, he could almost make out the old rascal's voice calling down the fury of the heavens upon his head. The figure transformed to the trim shape of Miss Wren, her skirts billowing around her ankles, hair lashing the air as she stood challenging the storm.

"Robbie, you're not even listening!" Geraldine's plaintive whining broke the spell that imagination had wound round him.

Irritated, he snapped his attention to where she sat hiding from the sun beneath her parasol. "What is it, Miss Scott?"

"Miss Scott?" She looked wounded. "I thought we were well past such formalities." She pouted in a way that someone had probably once told her was attractive. It looked too practiced to be spontaneous.

Robbie was not in the mood to flirt. Not with Geraldine at any rate. "What did you wish to tell me?"

She sighed. "I don't know what has gotten into you

today. You're no fun at all. I was merely asking what you were thinking offering to put on the Wren girl's dumpy little theatrical." She swatted at a mosquito. "I mean it's kind of you and all, but it will mean dreadfully boring hours for us all practicing it, and just think of all the poor people who have to sit through the wretched thing."

"I think it is very good."

She raised an eyebrow. "You can't mean it."

"I do." He took refuge in an indolent air, halting in his rowing and smothering a yawn. Not so subtly letting her know that she was boring him. "What I heard was original, witty and entertaining."

"It can hardly be original if she is copying Shakespeare." Chin high she stared off into the distance over Robbie's shoulder.

His grip tightened on the oars. "That's where you are mistaken. It is harder to be original, but it doesn't mean it can't be done."

"You're simply saying this to tweak me, aren't you?" A coy smile slid across her features. "It's all a prank?"

"No, Gerry. It's not. I'm in earnest."

"But you don't really expect us to have to put it on, do you?"

"I do."

She turned to wheedling. "Robbie, that's hardly fair. Shouldn't we all get a say in what we choose?"

"I'm the president of the theatrical society. I get to choose. But if you don't like my selection, of course you don't have to participate."

As he had hoped, that quelled her. Suddenly discontent with the day and the company, he put his back into rowing them ashore. The image of Julia's lively blue eyes and an almost smile as he had teased her kept pace, even as he rowed about the prettiest debutante of the season. It wasn't a good sign.

Chapter 3

Robbie inhaled as he stepped inside the cheerful pastel paradise of Wren's Ice Cream Parlor and Sweet Shoppe. Two ceiling fans kept the air moving, and set the sweet scent of cherries, rich chocolate sauce and velvety ice cream swirling all around him.

Nothing bad could ever happen in a place like this. Whimsical chalkboard signs identifying the day's specials took pride of place above a gleaming marble-topped counter that occupied most of the shop's length. A row of white wrought iron stools punctuated the counter, all but one of them claimed by customers. It all blended into a cool oasis away from the glaring August sun.

Once again Robbie longed for one of his cameras. Just a small one. Father would never see it, but these were moments worth capturing on film. Fleeting and sweet as ice cream, they might be, but there was also substance here. The innocent, ordinary pleasure that flavored life. He'd love to capture the sloppy, joyous grin on the face of a toddler who had managed to smear ice cream all over his face. Or the shy, smitten glances of a schoolboy who was peeking over the edge of his milkshake glass at a girl with a long fair plait hanging down her back.

And speaking of glances at pretty girls…he spotted Miss Wren behind the counter scooping a big helping of chocolate ice cream into a sundae dish. She topped it with a dollop of whipped cream and finished it off with a cherry, much to the delight of a small girl, perhaps seven or eight years old with fine blond hair and blue eyes wide with anticipation. She glanced at her mother for permission, then accepted the treat and dug in. Her first bite left a ring of chocolate around her mouth.

Miss Wren smiled at the little girl indulgently and exchanged a few words with the mother as she prepared a sundae for the lady. Her movements were graceful and sure. She accepted their coins and placed them in the cash register with a lively jangle of the bell, then glanced up.

When she caught sight of him, her newest customer, it was as if a shutter was pulled down over her soul, extinguishing the light in her eyes. Pain sliced through Robbie and he vowed in that instant to make her look at him differently.

Belatedly he removed his hat then approached the counter, mustering his most charming smile. "Good afternoon, Miss Wren."

"Mr. Malcolm." She nodded briefly. "Can I get you something?"

"Oh, a—how about an ice cream soda."

"What flavor?"

"Cherry?"

"Are you asking me or telling me?"

What was wrong with him? He was never this awkward. "Cherry, please."

"All right." She went into motion, her natural gracefulness asserting itself.

In a moment she slid him a tall, frosted glass turned pink by the contents and filled to the brim. He took a sip and murmured appreciatively. "That's good."

"That'll be ten cents."

He slid over a dime. "The theatrical society is supposed to hold auditions for the play tomorrow afternoon." He added, "They were already scheduled before we decided to use your play instead. Do you think you could manage to get away about four o'clock?"

"Get away?" Mr. Wren paused behind his daughter, wiping his hands on a tea towel.

Julia gave Robbie a glare that could have been patented as paint stripper. He had definitely—most definitely—said something wrong. Could it be that she hadn't mentioned the play to her father yet? He hadn't considered that it might be an actual inconvenience for her to direct the play. He shifted on his seat.

He straightened from his stool and extended a hand. "Mr. Wren, how do you do? I'm Robert Malcolm."

Mr. Wren accepted his handshake with a firm clasp of his own. "I know who you are, son." He might as well have said I know *what* you are. Suddenly, the reputation Robbie had built for himself as a ladies man didn't seem like much of a bragging right. "What I don't know is why and when my daughter will be trying to get away somewhere with you."

"Father!" Julia's cheeks glowed red.

Robbie moved in. After all, he did know something about soothing ruffled fathers. "It's nothing improper, I can assure you. Miss Wren has agreed to direct our amateur theatrical at the Park. It's her play in fact that we're putting on."

"She has, has she?" Mr. Wren looked at his daughter now. His walrus mustache twitched.

Julia examined a cherry stem that she had been shredding to bits. "I'm sorry, Pop. It all came up rather suddenly. I haven't had a chance to mention it to you before now."

No wonder she had given him that look. "I do hope you'll allow her to join us, sir. Her play is really very good."

"It is?" Mr. Wren paused. "And the folks up to the Park want to put it on?"

Robbie wasn't sure but he thought the older man smiled. "Yes, sir, we do. I think it will be a rousing success."

Mr. Wren looked at his daughter speculatively. "You want to do this?"

She glanced at Robbie.

He stared fixedly at a chalkboard sign over her shoulder, as if suddenly fascinated by the many varieties of malteds on offer.

"Yes, sir," she said.

Robbie decided never to play poker with her.

Late the next afternoon, Julia tried not to enjoy her first automobile ride. She still couldn't quite believe that Pop had acquiesced to her absence from the ice cream parlor so readily. The famous Malcolm charm must have made an impression. It was the only explanation she could think of. Particularly when he had agreed to allow Robbie to call for her in his auto.

Robbie passed through the gate with nothing more than a jaunty wave at the guards. No detailed checking of permits. She couldn't think of anything to say as the car slid up the steep grade that cut through untamed wilderness. They passed the race track and then the road leveled out. Just beyond that the view opened up to reveal many of the Park cottages.

Cottages.

She snorted softly.

The Italian laborers down in the town, crowded in their uniform rows of featureless hemlock cabins. Maybe those could be referred to as cottages. The gleaming homes nestled into the higher hills around them could be referred to as nothing but mansions.

Robbie looked at her curiously, but she didn't explain. The car skirted the edge of the lake and the breeze off the water caught her hair, sending strands whipping about her face, and threatening to tug off her hat. She clapped it on tight.

The Tuxedo Park Clubhouse swung into view. The great circular glass-enclosed veranda was the first feature that caught the eye. Robbie Malcolm didn't spare a glance for the impressive rustic architecture that blended so well with its wilderness setting. Julia couldn't help but sniff the air as she caught a whiff of the cedar shingles that had gone into its construction.

Mr. Malcolm parked the car and came around to open the door for her. Surprise flashed through her at this courtesy. True, he had assisted her into the car, but she was no Park lady. And yet here he was acting like a chauffeur.

She accepted Robbie's hand and stepped from his automobile. She felt like her body was still vibrating with the chugga-chug of the engine. His hand was warm, solid and had a stabilizing effect. Still she pulled away as soon as she gained her feet. Far be it from her to insist he wasn't attractive, but that didn't mean she had to fall prey to his attractiveness. Not like three quarters of the girls at the Park. Nope. She was made of sterner stuff and she would prove it.

Especially if she could make him stop being so nice and looking at her in that disconcerting way.

He led the way up the gray stone stairs and through the swinging doors and into the big hall. From there he took her to the clubhouse's grand ballroom with its circular shape and gleaming floors. A small cluster of chairs bunched before the stage. Mr. Malcolm strode to them, his heels clicking against the floor. She followed more slowly, trying not to sound like a horse clopping along. As he approached the chairs, he grinned and plucked a sheaf of paper from where a stack sat piled on the end seat.

He passed it over to her.

"What's this?"

"Your play. I had it typed up and mimeographed."

"You copied it?" Julia touched the first page with gentle, almost reverent fingers. Her words in print. They felt more real somehow and seemed to tremble as if alive. Or maybe it was she who was trembling. "Thank you."

He stepped closer than was strictly proper and gazed

down into her eyes. "My pleasure." His words were soft. Almost lost in the big room.

Julia's throat went dry, her hands damp. Goodness, he knew what he was about.

The door behind Robbie smacked open and Geraldine Scott swept into the room. The connection between them snapped. Julia took refuge in examining her script, panting and slightly panicky as if she were a rabbit released from a snare. She pretended not to notice, and definitely not to care, as Geraldine linked her arm through Robbie's and dragged him away.

Within a few moments, the room was replete with Parkies. None of them paid her any notice. Julia grasped the opportunity to examine the crowd as if they were exotic birds. The girls were all dressed expensively and in the height of fashion, with sweet summer colors and feminine frills. Julia glanced down at her own skirt of navy serge and her neat, striped shirtwaist. Then she straightened her spine. She hadn't come to compete. And even if she had, clothing was a silly thing to compete over. It wasn't as if they earned their dress allowances by some effort on their part. They'd simply had the good fortune to be born into the right households.

Robbie distributed copies of the play then took a position in front of the semicircle of chairs. "Thanks everyone for coming. As you likely know, we have decided to perform *A Tempest in a Teapot,* a modern retelling of Shakespeare's *The Tempest.* I've asked the play's author, Miss Wren, to be our director and she has graciously agreed." There was tepid applause. "Miss Wren, perhaps you could come up and tell us something of the play?"

All eyes shifted to her. Hands suddenly icy, she stood and joined him at the front, her pulse agallop. If there hadn't been so many witnesses she would have killed him. She cleared her throat. "The play begins in the midst of a labor dispute. A factory owner named Doug Anthony, his son and the plant manager are in a carriage which is besieged by angry strikers. They seek refuge and wash ashore, so to speak, at what initially appears to be a refuge—a walled reserve that contains only the fabulously wealthy and their servants."

There was an uncomfortable shifting in the seats.

Julia swallowed and glanced at Robbie. He gave a slight nod. She continued. "The reserve is the design of a man named Tom Prosper. He was once a wealthy tycoon like the refugees who seek sanctuary. Prosper has a daughter—Miranda. She knows that he was behind the strike, but she doesn't know why. During the course of the play it's revealed that Anthony swindled Prosper and drove him out of business. Miranda cares not. She and Anthony's son, Frank, fall in love. There is treachery, there are plots, but all comes right in the end, just as in the original. And true love reigns supreme."

"How quaint." Geraldine smiled then turned to Robbie and spoke in a stage whisper. "Do we really want to encourage talk of labor unions? I don't think it will be well received, Robbie."

Robbie moved on as if Geraldine hadn't spoken. "Thank you, Miss Wren. The point of the story is not the labor unions, though if such commentary makes you nervous, perhaps it is because it strikes close to home. But of course, this is what art should do. If it doesn't challenge you and move you to emotion, what is the point?" He rubbed his hands together. "All right, everyone take a few moments to review the scripts and decide which part you might like to tackle."

As pages rustled and heads bent over the scripts, Robbie put a hand on Julia's shoulder. "Nicely done."

She couldn't prevent the rush of warmth in her cheeks.

"There don't seem to be many female roles." Harriet Vines looked as if she'd sucked on a lemon.

"You could try for one of the male roles if you wish." Robbie's smile conveyed no mirth.

Harriet's mouth formed a perfect, scandalized O and she shook her head. "Robbie Malcolm, you are incorrigible."

He had Julia sit next to him at the apex of the half circle as the players auditioned for their parts. But it didn't take long for her to realize that this was merely an exercise in politeness; her preference was not consulted. As much as she wished to take offense at this, she was rather glad. She would no doubt have made enemies if she cast any sort of vote for one would-be thespian over another. Was it another form of consideration, or had he shut her out of the process for less altruistic reasons? She couldn't make up her mind.

In less than an hour, Robbie had parceled out the roles and collected the extra scripts. Then with a flourish of his hand and a command that they return on the morrow to begin practicing, he dismissed the cast.

They hustled out in whispering clusters. One or two glanced over their shoulders at Julia as they left.

He held the door open for her and she walked out with him, still in a sort of daze. It hadn't been so very terrible. The Parkies, for the most part had been decent to her. If she were honest, it was a bit thrilling to hear people reciting her words. As if she had created something of real value. She still could not quite grasp that her play, hers, the girl who scooped ice cream, was going to be performed. What if one of the residents enjoyed it and decided they wanted to produce it? Her play could be shown on Broadway. Julia put cold hands to suddenly flushed cheeks.

She had to rein in her imagination.

The summer sun was sinking lower as Mr. Malcolm handed her back into his auto. It took only three attempts before he got it rattling to life. Then he pulled away from the clubhouse with a loud backfire.

Julia slapped her hand down on top of her head before her hat could take to the wind.

"I think that went very well." He had to shout above the engine noise.

"Harriet Vines and Geraldine Scott still seem unhappy with the idea of the play."

"Sour grapes." He shifted a lever and there was a metallic screech that she was quite certain no machine should ever make. "Besides, I gave Geraldine the role of Miranda. And Harriet got Ariel. That should calm them down. They don't really care what play is mounted so long as they have the opportunity to be in the limelight."

Julia wasn't so sure, but he knew his fellow Parkies far better than she ever would.

The shadows grew long in the dying light, and Julia suddenly felt glad that she didn't have to walk all the way home from the clubhouse. It had been kind of Robbie to offer to drive her. She opened her mouth to say so when he yelled.

The world became a kaleidoscope of impressions all occurring at almost the same time. Something flashed at the edge of her vision. There was a pop and the sound of splintering glass. One of the headlamps winked out. The car swerved. Mouth grim, Robbie slammed on the brakes. Julia flew forward, her head cracking against something metallic. Her vision went red around the edges then faded to darkness.

Chapter 4

Gears ground as the Mercedes shuddered to a halt. Heart thundering in his ears, Robbie reached for Julia. She was crumpled, unmoving in the foot well. "God, help her," he breathed. The prayer sprang to his lips unbidden.

He eased her up toward him, trying to see where she was hurt. He wasn't entirely sure what had happened but something had come flying out of the night at them.

He managed to get her head in his lap and bent over her, trying to make out in the darkness where she was hurt. If only he could reposition his remaining headlamp. Teeth gritted, he explored her face gently with his fingertips. There was a spreading wet patch just below her hairline. He raised his hand, and as he did so the moon spiked through the clouds and he could see that his fingers were bloodstained.

"Are you having trouble with your motor?"

The voice startled Robbie and he straightened.

A young man approached the Mercedes from behind. Robbie recognized him vaguely as the good-looking Townie Julia had been with at the lake. At least that was who he thought it was. "We've had a bit of an accident."

The fellow rounded the car and stopped by the passenger side. He glanced at Julia and then all but leaped into the vehicle. "What did you do to her?"

The fellow began trying to drag her from the car.

Robbie pushed his shoulder. "Leave off. You're going to hurt her."

"Me? I find her bleeding in your car, and I'm the one who's going to hurt her? That's rich! But I don't care if you're some bigwig Parkie. I'm going to take her home."

Robbie wasn't about to relinquish his grip. "I'm taking her home. We were already on our way."

"I refuse to leave her alone with you."

"Then come along," Robbie snapped. "But I'm not letting you try to carry her home. It would take too long and she needs help."

As if to emphasize his point, Julia groaned.

The fellow climbed into the car, forcing himself into a seat which wasn't really made for three. He slid an arm under Julia's shoulders and pulled her to him. "I warned her that no good would come from consorting with your kind."

Had they been alone and with less at stake, Robbie would have called him out for that remark. As it was, he ground his teeth and released both sets of brakes, then shifted the lever on the steering wheel that increased the car's RPMs. At least he didn't have to get out and crank it up again.

It was a challenge to navigate by the light of the single lamp, making him feel lopsided and half-blind. But he managed to get them back on the road.

The only sound was the sputter-chug of the car's engine. Robbie had to admit, if only to himself, that it was a good thing the other fellow had come along. There was no way he could have held Julia still and kept her from getting hurt worse, while operating the car. He wished he knew the other man's name. Perhaps they could start over.

They reached the outskirts of the village. If he was going to ask now was the time. "Listen, I—" His words collided into some coming the other direction.

"What ha—"

They both stopped. Robbie waved a hand. "You go ahead."

"What happened? How did she get hurt?"

Robbie carefully strained all defensiveness from his tone. "I don't know exactly. It seemed like something flew at us. I swerved and braked and Julia hit her head. Whatever it was knocked out the left headlamp. But it all happened really fast."

"You must have been speeding recklessly. No regard for her safety."

Robbie shot the fellow a sideways glance. "Listen pal, I'm more than happy to fight with you, but don't you think we ought to get Miss Wren home safe first?"

The fellow had the grace to look sheepish. He fell silent again.

Julia groaned and shifted. Slight though the sound was, she immediately had the attention of both men.

The other fellow cupped Julia's cheek in one palm. Robbie wanted to sock him more than he had all evening.

"Julia?" Apparently he was on a first-name basis with her as well.

Another small groan from her.

A moment later, Robbie pulled up in front of the Wren home. Julia's eyelashes fluttered open. "Friedrich?" She winced and closed her eyes again.

Friedrich. Ha. That must be the fellow's name. Robbie hurried through the motions of turning off the Mercedes while Friedrich shifted gingerly from his seat and eased from the car. Seizing his advantage, Robbie leaned back in, and in a fluid motion slid one arm under her knees, and the other around her shoulders, and pulled her to him.

He couldn't resist a triumphant grin at Friedrich's fierce scowl. "Be a good fellow and get the door, would you?"

Something wasn't right. Julia blinked, her eyes heavy lidded, sluggish. Someone seemed to be trying to cleave her head in two. The pain radiating from a spot over her temple. And the whole world was moving, swaying as if the Park had slid into the lake. She was afraid she was going to be sick. Instinctively she burrowed into the closest solid surface. It was warm and smelled of cloves and mint. Nice. Safe. The scent soothed her. Settled her stomach.

What! Her eyes popped open.

Robbie Malcolm.

She pushed against Robbie's chest. "I can walk."

"Nothing doing."

She scowled, which hurt, and pushed again at his chest a little harder this time.

Robbie's voice was low, his breath warm against her

cheek. "Stop that. I don't want to drop you. That was a nasty blow to the head, and you're going to feel rotten enough without getting another."

She stilled and let her head rest against his shoulder. "I already feel rotten."

His arms tightened slightly and then his cheek brushed against the top of her head. He held her gently, securely, as he mounted the steps up to the porch.

A hard knock on the front door made her flinch, and she turned to see who was being so horribly loud. Friedrich? She'd been having a dream about Friedrich, or maybe she hadn't. She couldn't remember. Where had he come from?

Robbie shifted his weight. "Friedrich," his voice remained low. "If you bang like that again, I will give you the kick in the pants you have been begging for."

Julia pulled away slightly to look at Robbie's face, but there was no hint of humor there. He was in earnest. What was going on?

Pop opened the front door. His gaze swept past Friedrich to where Julia cradled in Robbie's arms. One eyebrow went up as he took in the sight. "Bring her in." He stepped aside so they could pass. "Put her on the sofa." He disappeared down the hall, leaving Robbie to lower Julia carefully to the cushions. He tried to make her lie down, but she sat up. Gingerly she probed the cut on her forehead, trying to figure out how bad it was. It hurt like all get-out, and she drew away fingers smeared with sticky wet blood.

Father returned with a cloth, a bowl of water and a small brown bottle. "What happened?"

Robbie explained about swerving to avoid something. It didn't take long.

"I'm all right, Pop." Julia took the damp cloth he was wiping her face with and did it herself. "Don't fuss."

Despite her protest, her father held her chin in his hand and peered at the gash over her right eye. He adjusted his spectacles, continuing his inspection. Robbie and Friedrich turned the same scrutiny on her. She could feel her cheeks growing warm, until at last she stood. The world spun a bit, but she locked her knees and managed to stay upright. "I'm just fine. I'm going to get some lemonade. Would anyone else care for some?"

Father took her place on the sofa. "You're going to have a shiner that will make every nine-year-old boy in the county jealous and a headache that'll make you feel like you've been trampled by a hippopotamus, or maybe wish you had been."

"A hippopot—" Julia gave the tiniest shake of her head. "The headache I already have. Lemonade?"

Robbie seemed to have realized he was still wearing his hat and snatched it off. "None for me, thank you." He held the brim in both hands.

Friedrich sneered at the Parkie and pointedly did not remove his hat. "You shouldn't be waiting on anyone in your condition. I will get you some lemonade."

Annoyance flashed through Julia at his presumption. "That isn't necessary, Friedrich."

"I insist. You should rest."

Julia had a sneaking suspicion that she really should rest. It stemmed from the wobbliness of her knees and the dizziness that was making the room waltz around her. Instead she straightened her spine. "You are our guest, Friedrich. I cannot impose."

Color suffused Friedrich's face and Julia braced for battle.

Before Friedrich could speak, however, Robbie interjected. He stepped forward and took Julia's hand in his larger, warmer one. "I'm so glad you are going to be okay, Miss Wren. Since that is the case, I will take my leave, unless…" He paused. "Mr. Wren, would you like me to fetch a doctor?"

Pop gave a brief shake of his head. "I don't think there's any call for that."

"Right. Well then, I…uh, I'll be on my way." He replaced his hat. "Good evening." His eyes met hers, as hot and dark as fresh coffee.

"Good evening," Julia murmured.

He stepped out into the hall before she remembered. "Thank you." Her words didn't carry very far. She doubted he'd heard. Slowly she sank back down onto the sofa.

She would make sure she told him next time she saw him.

Robbie loosened his collar as he jogged down the porch steps. His face was unaccountably hot. If he was smart he'd stay far far away from Miss Wren. The way she had looked at him—that half smile, those dewy eyes and flushed cheeks. He sighed. She was as fresh and unspoiled as…as…he couldn't think of a good metaphor. And since when did he think of metaphors anyway? He intended to see whether he could get closer to those sweet lips.

He gave the Mercedes's hand crank a hard turn. It chugged into life merrily with no consideration for his upset nor guilt over its part in the affair. He hopped in, his mind occupied with plans for the future. But first he had an errand.

The trip back to the accident site went more quickly than he'd have imagined. Before he knew it he saw the glimmer of glass in the light of his single headlamp. He pulled to the side of the road and got out. The normal night sounds of Tuxedo Park were subdued by the wheezy rattle of the car. But the smells weren't so easily overcome: the hot, black macadam of the road cooling now that the sun had gone down; the green and wild scent of the woods and the faint whiff of freshness on the breeze that heralded rain.

His shadow preceded him, long and narrow as he stepped into the road and squatted by the few shards of glass. He squinted in the poor light. This was the perfect time to try out his newest gadget. If only he had remembered it a bit earlier. Then they might have been gone before Friedrich arrived. He returned to the Mercedes and pulled from the toolbox the heavy flashlight that he'd bought in New York on a whim. He pushed the switch on the side of the fiber casing and the bull's-eye lens on the end began to glow.

He grinned. "'Let there be light.'" The wonders of modern science were endless.

He laid a piece of canvas on the ground and began collecting the fragments of broken glass. He didn't want some child or animal coming along and getting cut. At the edge of the slivers, his flashlight illuminated a larger object, and Robbie trained the light on it.

It was a chunk of brick. Dark red, bigger than his fist and unmistakable. He hefted it in his hand, testing the weight. He sighed and stared out into the shadowy woods. After a moment he stood and played the flashlight's beam all around the road. He had been hoping that it had been a confused bird that had flown into the lamp. But a brick certainly hadn't taken wing and flown. Accepting that, however, meant that he also had to accept the corollary. Someone had thrown it.

The question was, who would do such a thing, and why?

Chapter 5

Julia reclined against the pillow Pop had plumped up for her on the settee. He'd been hovering all morning and kept attempting to smooth a blanket over her. As soon as he stepped away she pulled it off and draped it over the back of the couch. It was too hot for blankets, and it wasn't as if she was an invalid.

Her headache was slightly less miserable than he'd predicted, but his worrying and fussing was far worse than she'd anticipated. She had given up trying to convince him that she wasn't incapacitated. Nothing would make him happy but that she should "rest." So she had spent most of her morning fidgety and bored on the settee. He wouldn't even let her read or write for fear it would make her head hurt worse.

In the absence of anything else to do that would help her ignore the ache, Julia's main occupation throughout the morning had been to keep her head still. It hardly hurt at all if she kept very very still.

A fly buzzed close to her face. She wrinkled her nose. Snorted a puff of breath at the fly, trying to give it the hint to move along.

It didn't take the hint. Lazily it buzzed nearer, taunting her. She cracked one eye open. Muttered imprecations didn't affect the hairy little monster in the least. She was about to take the drastic step of moving an arm to shoo the fly away when there was a knock at the front door.

Pop put down his paper and went to answer. Gingerly she sat up. She'd had enough lolling about, and any diversion would be welcomed at this point. Well, almost any diversion. She was still miffed at Friedrich for his overbearing manner and had no particular desire to see him.

But she shouldn't have worried, she knew Friedrich well enough to know he was miffed, too, and would keep his distance for a while. Instead, her guest proved to be Robbie Malcolm.

He looked as sober as she'd ever seen him. His features set like they were carved from granite.

Julia's heart gave a fluttery extra bump, which she studiously ignored. "Is something wrong?"

"You look dreadful."

"Diplomacy isn't your strong suit, is it?"

He blushed right up to the roots of his hair. "I'm sorry, I meant your injury looks dreadful. Not you of course."

Julia converted the laugh that burbled in her chest to a snort. "You can't even see it." It was true. Pop had bandaged her head so thoroughly that she looked like she was recovering from brain surgery rather than a bump on the forehead. "But never mind. Please sit down. To what do we owe the pleasure of your company today?"

"I came by to see how you are feeling."

"Not as bad as dire predictions made out." Julia smiled at Pop who was retrieving his paper. "I'm actually feeling quite well. Except for languishing for something to do."

A relieved smile cleared the last vestiges of stone and a light gleamed in Robbie's eye. "If you are up to it, I can take you to the rehearsal today."

"Well now, I don't know as that's such a good idea." Pop took his accustomed seat.

"Oh, please, Pop? I'm so dreadfully bored and I promise not to overexert myself."

He looked from her to Robbie. "Did you drive that fool contraption?"

"Yes sir, but I will be very careful, and we'll be sure to get back before dark."

"How you gonna make sure you don't have another accident?"

"I've had the headlamp replaced and I promise not to go over five miles an hour."

"Three."

Robbie looked pained, but he nodded. "Three."

"And you'll be back before dark?"

"Yes, sir."

Pop looked back to Julia who was clutching her hands in tight fists, silently praying that he would agree. He sighed, looking like a cornered man.

"All right."

Julia restrained a squeal of delight. She also refrained from jumping up and hugging his neck as she might have in other circumstances. As it was, jumping didn't strike her as the best idea.

Instead she rose sedately, noting with relief that the room didn't spin much at all. "I will get my hat and gloves."

In her room, Julia unwound the bandages Pop had wrapped around her head. There was no way her hat would even fit if she left them in place. Ignoring the twinge of sore muscles, she quickly redid her hair. It was still rather flat on one side, and the bruising looked livid. Sighing, she reapplied a fraction of the bandaging. Then she covered it with her hat. A few moments later, following several more admonitions from her father, Robbie helped her into the car.

It started with a rattle and a clang. *Did it shake this much yesterday?* Julia had the sinking sensation that she might have made a mistake, but then Robbie bounded up into the seat next to her, his grin making him blindingly handsome. And her headache receded again.

Julia gave Pop a little wave as they pulled away. Slowly. She'd been in buggies that went faster. "Do you think it would be faster to walk?"

Robbie looked at her askance. "Maybe."

She chuckled. "But then we wouldn't arrive in such fine style."

"An important point." His smile matched hers. "Style is paramount at the Park."

Goodwill thus established, Julia's headache ebbed a tiny bit more. It must be the fresh air. She settled back against the leather seat. They were going slow enough that she didn't even have to hang on to her hat.

Silence rested between them, but it wasn't the awkward, frustration-laden silence she often shared with

Friedrich. She felt no compulsion to maintain inconsequential small talk.

Just before it could grow strained, Robbie brought the car to a halt. "This is where the accident occurred last night."

Julia glanced around. "How can you tell?"

"I marked that stone right there."

Julia looked at where he was pointing to a broad chalk stroke on a rock next to the road. She glanced back at him.

"After I left you last night, I came here. The place was marked by the broken glass from my headlamp. And there was this." He reached down to the floorboard and brought up a chunk of broken brick.

Julia stared at his hand. "That was in the road?"

"Yes." He was watching her face.

Julia met his gaze. "What are you trying to say?"

"I think…" Robbie rubbed the back of his neck. "It seems that it wasn't an accident. Someone threw that rock at us on purpose."

She laughed. "Don't be ridiculous. Why on earth would anyone want to do such a thing?"

"I don't know. Is there anyone who is angry with you about something?"

Her mouth popped open. "I don't know what kind of person you think I am, but I can't think of anyone who could be angry enough with me that they'd try to hurt me. And besides that, it's hardly unusual to find a rock in the road."

"No. No it's not. And I didn't mean to offend. But surely you can't deny that something broke the headlamp."

"No. I guess I don't deny that. But it doesn't mean that anything nefarious is going on."

He nodded and allowed the car to move forward. His face stoic—unreadable.

Julia looked over her shoulder at the spot. "Besides, why would you assume it is someone angry with me? Why not someone angry with you?"

"I did consider that," he said stiffly. "But—"

"But what? You don't know the sort of low-class people I do. The only sort that could get up to that kind of mischief."

"Well my acquaintances don't tend to settle disputes through violence. We have other means."

"Meaning that mine do? Low-class we might be, but that doesn't mean we're savages. I would lay odds that if someone tried to harm us, it was one of your hoity-toity think-they're-entitled-to-anything-they-want Parkies. In fact, the way I've heard it, there are plenty of brothers and fathers who might want to teach you a lesson."

Their speed edged up. He looked over at her. "Townies gossip about us?"

Julia's cheeks stung with embarrassment. "You lot often forget we have eyes to see and ears to hear."

"What's that supposed to mean?"

"It means that I'd have to be blind and deaf not to know about your reputation."

"If you were a man—" He snapped his lips closed. His nostrils flared as he sucked in a big breath. After a long moment he said in a low voice, "Don't believe everything you hear."

Julia bit her lip. She shouldn't have let her fury take hold of her tongue. Now she would have to apologize, which was the last thing she wanted to do when she was still so mad. They pulled up before the clubhouse. The place reeked of money, just like Robbie. She needed to guard her heart and her tongue better. There was no sense fighting with him. She shouldn't know him well enough to fight.

Robert hopped out of the car and closed the door behind him carefully, then came around and opened her door. He stood stiffly, as if he was a footman and she the mistress.

"Listen, I—"

"You need say no more, Miss Wren." His jaw was still so tight it was a wonder he could talk at all. "You may not wish to see it, but the likeliest possibility is that a Townie threw that stone. I intend to find out who it was and see them punished."

Julia's chin climbed a notch. *Why couldn't she have been taller?* "You're wrong. If anyone, it was a Parkie, and I'll prove it."

Robbie hadn't been so angry in a very long time. Not since…he snorted to himself…not since he'd had that last row with Father. He couldn't even figure out why he'd become so mad. After all, over the past year or so he'd deliberately cultivated the reputation to which Miss Wren had referred.

He held the car door as she climbed out without accepting his proffered hand even though it was apparent to him that she was more in need of assistance now than she had been the day before, when the gesture had been a mere courtesy. Today she seemed ever so slightly unsteady. She swayed on her feet and gave a miniscule wince. Her hand made to move toward her head, but she arrested the movement. Except for the livid bruises over her eye, her face had gone pale again. A pang of regret speared him through the conscience. He shouldn't have pressured her to come to the rehearsal. And he definitely shouldn't have brought up his suspicions about the brick while her injuries were so fresh, and painful. The thought that someone might have targeted her for some reason could not have been welcome and was bound to worry her. Of course she lashed out.

She also had a point. Why should a piece of brick hold any particular meaning one way or the other? There was no reason it couldn't have been in the road for a full week before they came along. It was only the proximity to the glass that had made it in any way suspicious. He sighed, following her like an errant schoolboy trailing the teacher. It was probably some sort of morbid fantasy on his part. Certainly nothing he could really base any firm conclusions upon. Father would certainly have been in her camp on this whole subject.

And yet.

His theory did make sense. He stepped around Miss Wren to open the clubhouse door. He even had a prime suspect—Friedrich Whatever-his-surname-was. He had happened upon the scene all too conveniently for Robbie's taste. He had to admit that the fellow had seemed genuinely surprised and horrified at finding Miss Wren, but that could have been for any number of reasons. Maybe the fellow hadn't known that Julia was the person with him. Or maybe he had only intended to scare them, and hadn't intended real harm to anyone. Or maybe he was just surprised that Robbie hadn't been hurt, too. Something about the fellow smelled as ripe as moldy cheese.

Robbie opened the ballroom door as well and Julia

brushed past him leaving behind a faint scent of lemon and lavender. She stared straight ahead. None of the previous day's polite nods and half-surprised smiles of acknowledgment for the small service.

Robbie entered behind her to find that Harriet and Geraldine were already there. He paused. Somewhere just north of his belly button he could already feel an exasperated sigh building. These two were not noted for their timeliness and yet today they were early. It did not bode well.

Geraldine rose when she saw him and glided forward; every movement seemed calculated to display her many charms to best advantage. "Oh, Robbie. We heard all about your dreadful accident. Are you all right?"

"I'm fine." He pulled his head back a little as Geraldine reached to smooth a strand of hair from his forehead.

"You are so brave. But I've heard that an accident in an auto invariably causes injury to the neck and back."

Robbie's smile felt thin and dry as a cracker. "A little stiff. Hardly worth a fuss."

She reached to stroke his head again, and Robbie caught her hand. Behind them the door opened and several other cast members trooped in. Robbie stepped away, releasing Geraldine's hand as if they'd been caught in a compromising position.

"The one we should be worried about is Miss Wren. I'm afraid I've given her the most dreadful shiner."

Gasps went up from the newcomers and they moved in to get the full story.

Miss Wren looked distinctly uncomfortable in the limelight as she was engulfed by the surge, but the crew seemed genuinely concerned for her. At least some of them did. Mostly the fellows, if Robbie were any judge. A few of the girls hung back, their bodies held in postures of impatience that a Townie had upstaged them even for such a reason. Still he noticed that they did tilt their heads to better see Julia's injuries. *The cats.*

Except for Gwen Banks. Where she usually hung back, she pressed forward, a concerned look on her face. "Are you well enough to be up and about, Miss Wren?" She touched Julia's arm tentatively.

Julia smiled sweetly at the note of genuine concern and her shoulders seemed to relax. "I'm just fine." She leaned closer to Miss Banks. "It's not my first shiner, I'm afraid." Her stage whisper was pitched loud enough to reach every ear in the ballroom.

The other girls shared horrified grimaces.

"Really?" Gwen's eyes looked huge. "I've never had a...a shiner. Does it hurt much?"

The other fellows drew closer in, grins lighting their faces. "I've had more than a few in my day, let me tell you—"

It was as if the floodgates had opened. They were all swapping stories, most of them speaking over one another, and no one listening to anyone else's tall tales. As the hubbub rose, Miss Wren looked from one to the other, her smile faltering.

Robbie stepped in. "Lads. Lads." He raised his hands. "I'm sure all your mighty deeds are fascinating, but we have a play to practice for."

Geraldine stood at his elbow. "Robbie, dear, I do think that Gwen is correct. Julia doesn't look well. She shouldn't have to muddle along through an interminable practice when she should be resting." Her voice was light, cajoling.

Julia cut across his response. "As I said, there's no need, *Geraldine*." Her use of the first name was pointed.

Geraldine's mouth pinched in at the corners and he realized what she would look like in middle age.

Oblivious to any undercurrents between the two young women, Charlie Morton clapped Julia on the shoulder. "That's the spirit. You're brave as any of us, isn't she, boys."

She flinched, but her smile remained fixed.

"Hear, hear," someone called.

"Shall we begin?" Purposefully Julia moved to the stage. "I believe Charlie and Magnus are in the opening scene. Mr. Malcolm, do you wish them to be stage right?"

Grinning broadly, Robbie joined her. "You heard the lady, fellows. Hop on up and let's get to work."

Charlie gave him a light punch in the shoulder as he passed. "That's the first time I ever heard of Robbie Malcolm wanting to get to work."

Merry laughter greeted this riposte and Robbie chuckled along with them good-naturedly. He and Charlie traded a few more spars, while he maneuvered the would-be actors where he wanted them. And just like that, the last flickers of resistance to the idea of staging *A Tempest in a Teapot* dissipated like mist before the strength of the sun. He loved it when his plans worked out.

But still there was the issue of that rock. Did it have something to do with the play? He dismissed the thought as absurd.

Chapter 6

In spite of herself, Julia was enjoying the process of seeing her ideas come to life. She had braced for drudgery and ridicule, but except for Geraldine, no one seemed overtly hostile. As the production began to take form under Robbie's skillful hands, she could see that it did have potential to live outside her own imagination. And that... She sucked in a breath through her teeth. That was thrilling.

Charlie actually made a rather good Tom Prosper. Some of the others were pretty good as well. Geraldine in particular made a more believable and sympathetic Miranda than Julia had been prepared for. She had obviously been involved in a number of these theatricals. In fact, the more Julia watched her, the more it seemed apparent that the girl treated her entire life as a theatrical. Every movement and intonation was calculated for maximum effect on her audience. And, of course, there must always be an audience.

Watching the girl glide across the stage, Julia wondered idly whether Geraldine actually existed when no one was watching or if she simply ground to a halt. An automaton powered not by springs and gears, but by the attention of others.

Hmm, that could make for an interesting story idea. Professor Flitch had been encouraging her to *examine the human condition.* If she tied the idea of a woman who could only live in the presence of others to a man who—

"Hello?" A petulant voice sounded right at her shoulder. "Miss Wren, we're waiting."

Julia blinked.

Geraldine sighed heavily. "You see, Robbie. She's positively dazed. You really oughtn't have allowed her to stay."

Julia gritted her teeth. "I'm sorry, Geraldine, I didn't hear. What was it you needed?"

"I was beginning to think your senses had deserted you." Geraldine's voice was pitched to carry, and several of the Parkies turned to look. "Of course, I've thought that for a while."

There was no good response to such a comment. At least, no good response when one was trying to avoid a fight. But then why did it deserve a response? Julia bit back her retort, and simply kept looking with polite expectation at Geraldine, waiting for her to answer the question. Geraldine's pettiness had no power to wound unless Julia gave her credence. The knowledge was liberating.

With everyone watching her expectantly, Geraldine

was forced to continue on, though Julia suspected she had forgotten whatever question she'd asked to begin with. "Well now that you are gracing us with your attention again, could you please tell me whether I'm supposed to exit stage left or right?" Her tone was so snippy that the few side conversations going on died away.

Robbie plowed into the exchange. "Geraldine, we talked about this at the beginning of the scene. You exit stage right. Prospero, I mean Prosper, remains in place until the curtain closes."

"Fine. If you believe that will work."

"I believe it will work admirably."

"Fine."

There was an awkward pause.

Julia filled it. "Wonderful, then let's move on to the next scene."

The incident passed, but the knowledge of her imperviousness to Geraldine's opinion lingered, buoying her up. A tiny part of her wondered if this was a sign of some deficiency in herself. Shouldn't a lady value society's opinion? A much larger part decided that if society was all of a mind with Geraldine Scott, then she would be quite comfortable on the fringes, thank-you-very-much.

The boost of self-confidence was sufficient to see her through the remainder of the rehearsal. When the last would-be artistes had made their way from the ballroom, Julia put her hands on her hips and looked at Robbie, who was straightening a line of folding chairs. "I think that went well. They seemed more engaged than I thought they would be."

"Do you think so?" The corner of his mouth quirked

in a questioning half smile, as if he could not believe her naïveté.

"Yes." Julia's response was less confident than it had been a moment before. She marshaled her arguments. "Charlie and Gwen both seemed to get into their characters. And Geraldine did much better than I expected. She had actually practiced." Her confidence rebounding, she hurried on. "Even Harriet Vines, the poor stick, managed her lines." *Perhaps she shouldn't have added that last....* She wrinkled her nose. "I shouldn't have said that."

Robbie glanced down at her, eyebrow quirked. "Why not?"

"It wasn't very kind."

"She's not your friend."

She paused and looked up at him. "No. She's not."

"Then what does it matter?" He was offhand, but not flippant.

Julia's eyebrows rose and she stopped trying to straighten the pages of her script. "That's a real question, isn't it?"

He didn't reply, though the tips of his ears turned red.

Julia looked back down at the papers in her hand and managed to get the corners neatly aligned. "It doesn't matter if we are friends or not. It's the Golden Rule."

"Ah, the Golden Rule." His lips curled. "I thought that was akin to Father Christmas. An ideal designed to teach children to behave."

Julia tucked the pages under her arm and picked up her handbag. She didn't wait for him to open the door for her. "Perhaps it is to some people." She glanced back. "But I pity them."

It only took him two strides to catch up to her. "Misplaced pity surely, since it is the Golden Ruler who is likely to be taken advantage of."

"How is it being taken advantage of when it is a gift freely given?"

He changed tactics. "But if you think unkind thoughts, surely it is base hypocrisy to mouth sweet words." His smile was challenging; certain that he had gotten her with this sally.

Julia marshaled her thoughts as they moved through the big hall. A huge stone fireplace dominated the room, unlit at this time of year, but several of the cast members congregated before it in comfortable leather couches. Geraldine, among them, watched her and Robbie as they passed. He didn't seem to notice.

Robbie offered her his arm at the head of the stairs, and this time she accepted. She had her answer ready. "The Golden Rule isn't about words, it is about actions. The fact that I may not like someone doesn't preclude me from being respectful and kind. And besides, feelings are fickle things. By treating someone well regardless of their response to me, I leave the door open for the relationship to improve. Treating someone poorly robs me of a potentiality, and I refuse to do myself the injustice."

Robbie laughed as he swung his motorcar's door open for her. "I yield." His voice was full of mock surrender. "You have bested me in the debate."

A little thrill skirled through her. No matter how persuasive she thought her argument, Friedrich never conceded even that she had scored a point in a debate, much less that she had won. Robbie's concession was not only given, but seemed ungrudging and good-humored.

He shut the door gently behind her. "I ought to turn you loose on my father. He'd be no match for you."

The rush of Julia's heart slowed. Soberly she asked, "Do you have an ongoing debate with your father?"

He crossed around to his side of the car. "Everything I do causes a debate with my father." The humor was gone from his eyes and he shut his door pointedly.

Should she probe further or would he think she was prying? She studied his face a moment as he worked the ignition. He ignored her gaze as he fiddled with switches and levers.

"Oh, don't fret. It's no secret. Everyone in the Park knows." He looked over his shoulder to make sure the way was clear and began to back the car out.

"I'm not part of the Park."

"No you're not." He looked at her then, and the smile returned to his lips. "Would you like to go into town with me tomorrow evening and take in a real theatrical production?"

Julia's mouth sagged open and she blinked at him.

His hand slid over hers, caressing gently. The heat of his palm oddly made her shiver.

By town he meant New York City. The idea was completely foreign. Who trotted off on a whim to take in a show in the middle of a workweek? But she loved the theater and it wasn't really that far. Not with a car at your disposal. But no. No she couldn't do such a thing, not alone with a young man. Cheeks burning, she pulled her hand free. "I don't think so. I'm only a Townie, but that doesn't mean I'm willing to sacrifice my reputation for the sake of your attentions, Mr. Malcolm." She put as much chill in her voice as she could, hoping he wouldn't realize that she had, for the briefest instant, considered the idea.

He placed both hands on the steering wheel and the car moved forward at a sedate speed. "I won't foist my attentions on you, Miss Wren. I simply thought it would be fun." Some of the starch seemed to go out of his spine. "The Park girls don't debate as well as you. I make the most ridiculous pronouncements and their only response is to blink and flutter their eyelashes." He laughed ruefully. "I never know if they think I'm a dolt or if they can't summon enough mental energy to consider me a dolt."

"Miss Scott doesn't seem to think you are a dolt."

He shook his head. "I never can tell. But you—" He grabbed her hand and raised it to his lips then released it again just as quickly. "You would keep me on my toes. It would be no fun at all to play the dolt around you."

Julia's hand tingled. His grip had been tight, not painful, but not gentle either. The press of his lips against her hand, hard and almost fierce. Her heart raced and her cheeks burned. She didn't know what to do. She clasped her hat to her head to keep it from flying away. "You told my father you wouldn't go faster than three miles an hour."

Instantly the car slowed as he removed his foot from the accelerator. The slower pace didn't help her spinning thoughts though. They were all atumble. He'd left a string of broken hearts in his wake, and she refused to be one more conquest.

Desperate for a distraction she cast about for another topic of discussion. "Why are you and your father at odds?"

He raised an eyebrow. "Do you really care to know?"

"I asked."

"The biggest reason is because I don't want to go into the family business."

"What is the family business?"

He snorted. "Making money."

"Isn't that what all businesses are—"

"We trade stocks. We don't create anything. We purchase pieces of businesses and trade them and buy other pieces. It's pointless really."

"What would you rather do?"

His snort this time was full of self-derision. "Something even more pointless."

Robbie waited for her reassurance that his ambition couldn't possibly be pointless. He'd made his revelation before and it had followed the same path every time. He would tell a woman, and she would try to look as if she hadn't said something silly. And finally would come the reassurances that it would make a fine hobby.

But Julia simply waited, looking expectantly at him.

"I want to take pictures."

"Like a photographer? What kind of pictures?"

No one had yet asked him that question. Usually they were far too distracted by the frivolousness of the idea. Still, they would get on track again in a minute. His attempted explanations always made things worse. Oh well. He threw his hand all in.

"Not like a portrait studio. I want to go out in the streets and capture real life. I want to go wherever things are happening and record it. Journalists do it with words. But, as the saying goes, a picture is worth a thousand words, right?"

Instead of looking at him askance she nodded thoughtfully. "Something like a war correspondent then? Like Mathew Brady in the Civil War?"

"Yes. Exactly. I can't believe you know who Mathew Brady was." His heart gave a surge upward and he had to ease off the gas pedal again. "Only not just with wars. With the comedies and tragedies and dramas of everyday life. I want to capture individual stories and share them with the world." He winced. Why had he allowed himself to get excited? To reveal so much.

She didn't seem to notice. She was looking thoughtful. "The newspapers are using more pictures than they used to. I'm sure they have realized that the pictures give life to a story. I think they will use more and more over time. Magazines too will use more photos than drawings one day." She cocked her head. "What is your father's objection?"

Robbie sighed. "They are manifold. He wouldn't care if I snapped a few shots of the family on holiday. But he doesn't think a hobby should be given the same rank as a career. Most especially since it is unlikely to pay much."

"Are you good at it?"

"At taking photographs?"

She nodded.

Robbie had a feeling that false modesty wouldn't satisfy her. "I think I am actually. And…I…there's something almost sacred about it. I can't explain, but I feel more alive when I have a camera in hand."

Her smile was knowing. "I feel the same when I have a pencil and a clean sheet of paper. Like I'm doing what I'm meant to do." Her gaze held him steadily. "So what are you going to do?"

He'd been right. She was completely different and this was completely uncharted territory. He cast her a sidelong glance. "Do? There's nothing I *can* do. He's threatened to cut off my allowance if I so much as pick up a camera again. He has ordered me to cast aside *all that nonsense.*" He took his hands off the wheel to imitate his father's commanding gesture as he had made the pronouncement.

"I see."

Her words were neutral, but Robbie felt the sting of indictment. "What does *that* mean?"

She looked at him wide-eyed. "Nothing."

"You think I'm a milquetoast for letting him control me by tightening the purse strings, don't you? Well, what about *Honor your father and mother?*"

She touched his elbow, drawing his eyes briefly away from the road. "I think that, or you think that?"

The gentle words felt like a knife wound. Thankfully they had arrived at her home. He parked, and blindly made his way around the car to let her out. He just wanted to be alone. Why had he ever thought that putting on her play would be a bright idea? It was more trouble than it was worth. "Do you think you can make it to the rehearsal tomorrow without me? I have other obligations in the afternoon."

"I'll be there." Her voice was calm. She straightened, and her five-foot frame seemed more imposing than he remembered. "Robbie, I didn't mean to hurt you. Just…I don't think that honoring your father is necessarily the same as slavish obedience. Not when you're an adult. You have a responsibility to God and yourself as well. If He has given you a gift… Well, only you can decide

if the security of your father's fortune is more important to you than your dream."

She left him staring after her as she climbed up the
stairs and entered the tiny house. She didn't look back.

Chapter 7

Julia thrust aside her blanket for the umpteenth time. It was too hot and she was too wrought up to sleep. Pop had thought she looked peaky when she got home and sent her to bed early. Now it was the middle of the night and she was wide awake.

Abandoning her tussle with the bed linens, she slipped downstairs. What she needed was a nice cool drink of something. That would surely wash away the memory of the burn of Robbie's lips against her skin, and the heat of his eyes between her shoulder blades as she had walked away.

Every story she'd ever heard of him warned her to shy away. He was a fox and she was a plump, juicy hen. Foxes were sly and plausible. They wove stories and made the chicken forget that it was just a chicken.

And yet, today, Julia was certain that she had glimpsed the substance of the real man beneath his veneer of charm and sophistication. He had a core that was perhaps softer than his outer layer would lead one to believe. Or actually, as she thought about it, it seemed the reverse was truer. There was more substance to him than she had originally suspected.

But wasn't that exactly what the fox wanted the chicken to think?

And what had she been doing, thinking that it was all right to offer unsolicited advice. She hated it when people did that to her. She didn't know his father, or all the details of his situation. She'd wanted to say something to challenge him and make him think. Maybe it would help him to see his problem differently. But she had a sneaking suspicion that she had been more interested in sounding profound than in helping Robbie. His admiration for her intelligence was a little intoxicating.

Did foxes encourage chickens to think?

She was so confused. She plopped down at the table with her glass of lemonade from the icebox then raised the glass and let it rest against her forehead. Using her other hand she pulled the hair away from her sticky neck. A longing to go swimming in Tuxedo Lake welled up. She quickly shoved the idea down. That line of thinking had landed her in this mess to begin with.

The scent of smoke reached her nostrils. Listlessly she wondered who in their right minds would start a fire on such a night? Maybe old lady Firelli? She wasn't quite right anymore. She could be thinking of a snowstorm she survived as a child.

The creak of wood sounded from somewhere nearby and Julia raised her head. That had come from outside. On the porch maybe? Was there someone out there?

She slipped into the hall, every movement slow and

measured. If there was an intruder she didn't want to alert them to her presence.

An orange flicker winked along the wall, and she moved more quickly. She could hear the whisper of fire. All thoughts of intruders vanished in the face of this new threat. She flung open the front door and found a flaming bundle of papers on the porch.

As she watched, the top page blackened and curled. It was the title page of her play.

Instinctively she recoiled from the flames, but then stepped forward again and flung her lemonade on the pile. It hissed and steamed, but didn't sputter out. It had hold of the wooden porch, as if the porch had been set on fire and the papers placed on top as added fuel. Or perhaps a warning?

Julia dashed back down the hall to the kitchen. She pumped water furiously into a basin. "Pop!"

He stumbled down the stairs as she raced back through the hall, water sloshing with every step.

"What?"

She didn't pause to respond as she flung the water at the fire.

It had gained ground while she was in the kitchen. Scorch marks spreading out and away from the center in every direction. She hurried back down the hall, her father on her heels. This time he pumped the water.

"Grab the bucket."

She obeyed, snatching a mopping bucket from the back of the pantry and trading him for the now full basin. Once more she sped down the hall and flung her burden at the fire.

This time the fire reared back, wounded and sputtering. It hadn't gained much ground. She turned and fled back to the kitchen for the bucket. It was nearly full when she made it to the kitchen and her father passed it off to her.

The last bucket did the trick. With an angry hiss and a burst of steam, the fire died. Livid red embers speckled the charred and smoking center of the porch, threatening to erupt again.

Julia stared at the pile of ash in the center of the wet smoky mess. Had it really been her play?

Why would anyone do something like this? Her mind sifted through possibilities as her finger probed the hot black cinders, looking to see if it had all been consumed. A thoughtless prank or a vicious one? A warning? But about what? And why? She was a nobody and a nothing. Why would anyone bother with her at all?

Maybe that was the key. Maybe one of the Parkies was angry that a nobody like her was being promoted at the clubhouse. Maybe they were angry that her play was being produced. But who could possibly care so much about an amateur theatrical? It was absurd.

Her father appeared at her shoulder. Water sloshed over the rim of the basin in his arms. "Back away from that, Julia, it could still be dangerous."

She complied absently. There wasn't so much as a single legible scrap of paper left anyway.

He doused the final smoldering remains and then stared down at the charred circle. "What happened?"

A clanging bell echoed down the street. Someone had called the fire department. Julia glanced down at herself. "I better go put on something more presentable."

Father caught her arm as she turned, his eyes brimming with concern. "Do you know what happened?"

She shook her head. "I wasn't sleeping well so I came

down for a glass of lemonade. Then I smelled smoke and when I checked, I found the fire."

"Why would someone do this?" The hand with the basin in it dangled at his side. He scratched the back of his neck with the other. His brow was furrowed, his glasses crooked on his nose. "I can't think of anyone I've offended lately."

"I don't know, Pop." She shook her head. It was on the tip of her tongue to mention the play, but she held back. She didn't actually know anything, and saying something would only make him worry more. He'd probably forbid her to have anything more to do with it, and if that occurred then Friedrich and Minna would be out of the jobs they both needed very much. The fire department's clamorous bell grew ever louder. "I need to at least put on my wrapper, unless you want all the firemen to see me in my nightdress."

He jerked his chin toward the door. "Go on."

Julia climbed the stairs slowly. With all the reeling her mind had been doing in the past few days, she was going to get permanently dizzy. She took her time putting on her dressing gown, some distant part of her mind registering the black streaks her fingers were leaving on the soft cloth, but unable to summon enough energy to care overmuch. She wove her smoky-smelling hair into a quick plait, and then paused to put on slippers before making her way downstairs again.

Father stood on the porch talking to the firemen.

The general consensus seemed to be that some village lads had been playing a prank that had gotten out of hand. None of them bothered to ask Julia any questions. Within a few moments they were gone, and with their departure, the small crowd of neighbors wandered off home as well.

Numbly, she followed her father inside and endured a dose of awful-tasting medicine before retreating back upstairs again. In the bathroom she caught sight of her smudged face and black eye. She washed carefully and then all of a sudden the smoke smell made her nauseous. She chucked her clothes and drew a bath. Tears ran down her cheeks as she scrubbed at her skin and hair to get rid of the clinging scent.

An hour later she tumbled into bed. The medicine made her woozy and yet she still couldn't seem to sleep. She could not dismiss the fire as a prank so easily. But what could she do about it?

Chapter 8

Robbie pressed hard on the gas, pushing the engine into doing nearly its limit. He sped down the road at nearly fifty miles an hour, heedless of the stares and curses he was garnering.

The Tuxedo Park gates loomed close and he slowed marginally as he prepared to pass through. It looked clear. He accelerated again and flew past the guard post, but as he did, a slim figure in discussion with the on-duty guard caught his eye.

He slammed on his brakes. The tires spun and the car slewed sideways. He corrected the skid and then slammed into reverse. One arm flung over the seat and watching over his shoulder, he drove backward to the guardhouse.

Julia and the guard both watched him openmouthed.

The guard spoke first as he drew near. "You need to slow down there, Mr. Malcolm. The speed limit is eight miles an hour in the Park."

"Sorry, I was in a hurry." Dismissing the guard he turned to Julia. "Are you all right? I heard about the fire."

"Ah, was that your house?" The guard seemed determined to insert himself into this discussion.

"I thought you were busy this afternoon." Her reply was cool.

Robbie ignored the question. "I was coming to check on you."

She spread her arms. "Well, as you can see, I'm fine."

"Did you get that black eye in the fire, miss?" the guard asked.

"No. That was from a motor vehicle accident with Mr. Malcolm here." She smiled sweetly at the guard.

The fellow hooked a thumb into his belt loop and stood tall. "This is what I was saying. You need to slow down. You could kill someone tearing around the countryside like some sort of maniac."

Robbie's jaw clenched so tight he thought he heard the bone creak. "I appreciate the advice." He reached across and opened the door. "Come on, Julia, I will drive you to the clubhouse."

"That's kind, but it's not necessary. I know you had other pressing business."

"She's your guest is it, Mr. Malcolm? She didn't have a work pass, so I was just telling her I couldn't let her in."

"Add her to my guest list permanently," Robbie said. Once more he half turned away from the fellow, trying to make it known that he wasn't interested in a conversation with the man.

"Sure enough. Sure enough." The man pulled a board from the desk and laboriously inked in Julia's name.

Julia meanwhile seemed as intent on ignoring Robbie, as he was on ignoring the guard. "Is there anything further you need?" She tilted her head prettily at the guard.

"Nope." He stared at the clipboard and shook his head. "No, ma'am. I think we're all set here." He gave her a wide grin. "You ever have any trouble getting through, just tell 'em that Ernie said it was okay."

"Thank you, Ernie."

"Good, well, I'm glad we got that sorted." Robbie couldn't quite keep the aggravation from his voice. "Now do get in, Julia."

She raised an eyebrow at Robbie's coaxing. "Are you certain I'm not inconveniencing you?"

"Yes." He blew a raspberry. "You know I was making an excuse."

"I know." She opened the door and slid in. "I just wondered if you would admit it."

Robbie hooked an arm over the seat and backed the car up until he had room to turn around. "I've never been good at dissembling."

"That's not the worst fault in the world."

"Depends on who you listen to."

"I suppose it does." Once again, an impish smile made her features light up. But there were still shadowy smudges beneath her eyes.

Robbie pulled off the macadamized road. "Tell me about the fire."

She glanced over her shoulder, as if fearful. "We can't stop here, someone will see, and draw 'conclusions.'"

"Well, we can't really talk at the clubhouse. Far too many eavesdroppers. If it makes you feel better, I'll hop out and tinker with the engine. No one will think a thing." He swung out of the car and took off his jacket, rolling up his sleeves.

She started laughing.

It was a sweet, liquid sound. Cool and refreshing as a brook. He dove into the trunk and pulled out a wrench then walked to the hood. He waggled his eyebrows. "Now I'm official."

He yanked it open and peered inside at the metallic jigsaw puzzle. "Now about that fire?"

"I don't know what you heard, but it was never life threatening or anything." She climbed from the car and came to peer beside him at the engine. "It was contained to the porch. Pop and I were able to put it out with a few buckets of water."

He refused to be distracted by the smell of her. Something citrusy but with the sweetness of lavender. Sort of light and deep all at once. Combined with the dusty sun-baked scent of August it was intoxicating. He cleared his throat. "How did it start? Wait. How did you know it had started?"

Julia explained about waking up thirsty. "When I smelled the smoke, I went to see what was wrong."

"As simple as that, huh?"

She shrugged and bent to peer more closely at some fascinatingly grimy bit of machinery.

Robbie pulled back. Something was not quite right. He was sure of it. Had been sure of it since he heard about the fire. "How did it start?"

"I didn't see it start."

"An excellent attempt at avoiding the question."

"Avoiding?" Her eyes were wide and innocent. And very blue. So very blue.

"Yes, avoiding."

She sighed. "I don't know anything for sure."

"But you suspect something."

"I don't know what to think, honestly."

He turned his back on the engine and leaned up against the car, arms crossed.

She sighed. "It was a pile of papers that was burned on the porch. I...I think it was a copy of the play."

"Your play? *A Tempest in a Teapot* you mean?" He straightened. "Why would anyone do that?"

She raised her hands in a helpless gesture. "It doesn't make any sense. Who would care so much about a silly little amateur production of a no-name play?"

He put his palms out. "Let's not get personal."

"You know what I mean." She batted at his arm. "Do you think it's possible? Could someone really be so deranged?"

Robbie grew serious. "I hate to admit it, but I do."

Her shoulders sagged. "Me, too." She sounded rather as if she were relieved, like she had confessed some sin and found forgiveness rather than condemnation. "But then which of the Parkies hates the idea of doing my play so much that they would attack me for it?"

"Parkies?" He snorted. "No Parkie would get so worked up about it. It's just a play, we did one last summer, and we'll do another next summer. It must have been a Townie." As he spoke he saw her back straighten with an almost audible chink as a rod of iron drew her tall.

"And what would a Townie have to gain? Most of them probably don't even know that my play is being put on."

"Don't kid yourself. The Townies know everything

that is going on in the Park, whether we want them to or not."

"But none of them have any stake in the play. Who among them would care one way or the other?"

"You said yourself it has to be someone who is deranged."

"Oh, I see." Her hands landed on her hips. "Only we of the 'lower orders' are susceptible to madness. You bluebloods in the Park are immune."

"That's not what I meant."

"What did you mean?" she asked with narrowed eyes.

Robbie swallowed. His throat suddenly felt parched as he realized how much he cared what she thought of him. "Hear me out."

She crossed her arms. "I'm listening."

"The first person I thought of was your friend Friedrich." Her mouth popped open and he raised a finger. "Just listen. Please. It's pretty clear that he doesn't like us Parkies much. And he was unhappy when you agreed to let us perform your play. You should have seen the look he gave me when I suggested it. I came within a hair of bursting into flames. I think he would have rather been sacked than see us put on your play."

"That doesn't mean he'd set my house on fire. He'd be much more likely to go after you."

"Perhaps by chucking a brick at my car as I'm driving?"

"Yes." She gave an impatient shake of her head. "No! He's not a violent person."

"Are you saying that he didn't try to talk you out of allowing us to use the play?"

"He did." Her smile was wry. "He tried to convince me that the Parkies are unworthy of my genius—"

"Well, he and I can agree upon that point." Robbie sketched a bow.

She rolled her eyes. "I just can't picture it. Friedrich is passionate and idealistic. He sees everything in black and white. And he can never admit that he might be wrong, which can be hugely frustrating. But I don't think he'd ever deliberately put me in danger."

Robbie decided to stop pressing his luck. He raised his hands in surrender. "All right, but remember, he came along very conveniently the other night."

"He was probably on his way to visit his mother."

"So late?"

"She has cancer. He can go see her only on his half day off or if he gets leave of his employers. And that's only when they don't need him. As a chauffeur, that tends to be late."

Unwillingly, Robbie imagined what it would feel like to have to beg for time off to spend with his dying mother. He inhaled through his nose. He couldn't let sympathy blind him to possibilities. "Then why didn't we see him on the road?"

"There could be any number of reasons." She looked at her wrist, as if expecting to find a watch. "We're going to be late."

"They won't start without us."

"Not on my play. But if you're not there to impose your will they may mutiny and go back to *A Doll's House*." Her tone was a bit more acerbic than he would have liked.

Robbie snorted, playing along as if she had indeed

made a joke. "They would never put forth the effort to learn two sets of lines."

She smiled in response, but he sensed resolve brewing behind her placid demeanor. He opened the door for her and she settled into the seat with a graceful twitch of her skirt. He caught another whiff of her scent and for an instant his brain seemed to derail again.

With an effort he wrenched his thoughts back on track. "Are you planning something?"

Wide-eyed she stared up at him. "What do you mean?"

Stiffly he walked around the car and climbed in. "You're still certain that whoever lit that script on fire was a Parkie."

"I'm not so close-minded as to think that's the only possibility." She stared pointedly ahead. "But I think it is more likely."

He pressed the accelerator and the car leapt forward with a jerk and a grinding of gears. "Well, I still think Friedrich is the more likely culprit."

"We shall see."

"You *are* planning something."

She shrugged. "I'm just going to ask a few questions."

He had a strange, seasick feeling in his gut. Someone should get to the bottom of this. But if she was going to ignore the obvious, it would be up to him.

Julia came close to grinding her teeth. Only desperate fear of the dentist's chair restrained her. She was just about tired of overbearing, opinionated men. At least Robbie hadn't tried to order her not to talk to the Parkies. Friedrich certainly would have. But then, Robbie probably didn't care about her as much as Friedrich did. The thought felt rough around the edges and about two sizes too big for the space she wished to allot it. Which didn't make sense. Why should she care one whit what Robbie Malcolm thought about her? They hardly knew each other, and after this play was done, they wouldn't have any further contact unless he had a hankering for ice cream and came to the shop.

She needed to remember her real friends and her real life. She would prove to him that Friedrich wasn't the one behind the fire or the shattered headlamp. She folded her hands primly in her lap. It would do him good to know that Parkies weren't perfect and neither was he.

Having made up her mind, Julia decided she could be gracious. She glanced over at Robbie. He was scowling ferociously and glaring at the road like it had affronted him. On second thought, the silence was fine. They didn't really have anything to discuss anyway.

At the clubhouse the entire cast of the play milled about on the lawn. They moved toward the car as Robbie and Julia arrived. Once more she was the center of attention, everyone agog to hear about the fire. Inside her gloves, her hands grew damp.

She should have anticipated this. Already she was the Tame Townie, a sort of sideshow freak attraction, but somehow she kept finding new ways of becoming even more of a spectacle. Why had she even come? Dying of boredom was preferable to dying of embarrassment. She should have stayed home.

Too late for regrets.

Chin high she waited for Robbie to come around and open her door. She braced for the impertinent questions she was sure would come. And if she had to endure their questions, well, that could cut both ways. As it was, knowing Friedrich was suspected, she could try to find out who was really behind these incidents. It could even be one of the beautifully turned out debutantes or dashing dandies clustering around the car. But which one?

Chapter 9

Julia told her story as briefly as possible, which wasn't all that brief since people kept interrupting.

"It was a prank. That's all." She smiled. "Hooligans looking for mischief."

"I thought it must be some sort of Townie foolishness. I don't know why the villagers don't keep better control of their children." Geraldine turned pointedly and headed for the stairs.

Several Parkies drifted after her, and with the inertia broken, Robbie was finally able to corral the swarm of thespians and lead them into the ballroom. Inside he began the rehearsal at once, ordering people about as if he had been born to it. Which, come to think of it, he had.

Worried that she might start them all buzzing again, Julia hung back along the edges of the great circular room, while the Parkies clustered around the stage to receive their marching orders. She inhaled deeply of the great ballroom's distinctive odor—wood polish, and high hopes, and the ghosts of innumerable flowers.

It was her turn to ask questions. But where to start? She surveyed the Parkies. Someone had to know something. Assuming there was something to know. But who would know, and who would tell her if they did?

She was starting to make herself dizzy.

As the first of the actors took their places, she stepped up beside Charlie. He was as good a place as any to start. He was one of the most popular Parkies and easily one of the friendliest. "You're doing a wonderful job as crotchety old Tom Prosper."

"Thanks." A wide grin split his face and he leaned close as if he were imparting a secret. "I'm just imitating my old man."

She laughed. There was something disarming about Charlie. "He must be quite the handful."

"You have no idea." He shook his head ruefully.

Distracted by this tantalizing sideline, curiosity got the better of her. "It must be a common theme at the Park. I understand that Robbie has difficulties with his father, too."

Charlie grunted. "Robbie's dad is in a class all his own. They go at it hammer and tongs." His voice carried the faintest whiff of pity.

"It must be hard on him." They both watched Robbie as he showed Tommy Beyers how to move through his scene for the eighty-second time. Julia pressed a little more. "Has it always been that way, or just since Robbie decided he wasn't sure about going into the family business?"

Charlie pursed his lips. "Always. They're too much

alike, and too different all at the same time. Bound to clash. But it's gotten worse since he broke that bit of news."

"Robbie seems pretty unhappy about the situation."

"He'll come around. He must know that his picture taking is all right for a hobby, but it isn't as if it could make a career. Not for men like us. I think his dad is trying in a ham-handed sort of way to make him see that."

Julia glanced to where Robbie was now demonstrating for Magnus how to make it look as if he was fighting without actually landing a blow on the other actor. If even his closest friends espoused his father's opinions he must feel pretty isolated.

"I'm glad you're all right. When I heard about the fire this morning, I was worried."

Still thinking about Robbie, she brushed the polite comment away. "That's kind. But it was only a prank." What was she doing? She needed to talk about this. Julia snapped her attention back to Charlie.

Luckily he was continuing. "You never can tell with gossip. Sometimes they've got people fitted out with their burial wreaths and the poor soul only has a cough."

"Did you hear I had died?"

"No. No. Just that there was a fire and no one knew how you were."

"I'm surprised that the people of the Park knew at all. I didn't know the Parkies took any interest in the village."

"Oh, we heard all right. We've got men in the fire brigade, too, you know. So we're always interested if there's an alarm."

Well so much for her idea that the gossip would have had to be started by the vandal and all she needed to do was follow the trail back to the original source. Julia wrinkled her nose trying to figure out where to take the conversation next. This was a lot harder than it sounded in mystery novels. "It's nice of you—"

"There's my cue." He bounded out onto the stage.

Sighing, she wandered over to her usurping robber baron, Anthony, the man who had displaced poor old Tom Prosper. "What do you think, Paul?"

"Huh?" He started as if she had woken him from a nap.

Her conversation with Paul was less than enlightening. She spoke to several of the other cast members, but either no one knew anything, or they were too clever for her oh-so-subtle questioning.

A few of the girls who had previously been cordial shot sideways glances at her, but when she approached they were all very busy. The reason wasn't lost on her. Julia caught Geraldine's smug little smile as she turned away to point out something in the script to Robbie. Despite their reluctance to converse, Julia had the feeling that it wasn't really personal, but a matter of principle. She didn't belong with them. She knew it, and they knew it. There was no point in striking up friendships that could only be curtailed by their respective stations.

Still, despite their coolness, none of them made her feel threatened. Not even snobby Geraldine Scott. Was it possible Robbie was right and that the troublemaker was a Townie?

No. She refused to think that Friedrich would ever try to hurt her or even scare her. He was her friend, even when they didn't see eye to eye.

Even if he could be overbearing.

Even if she wanted to throttle him much of the time.

Busy with her attempted investigations, Julia could hardly believe it when the cast began drifting away, and she realized that the rehearsal had ended. She didn't know if Robbie meant to drive her home again, but she thought the walk would feel good. She looked around for Robbie so she could tell him. She spotted him over to one side of the stage in close conversation with Geraldine. Forgetting herself for a moment, Julia watched. A knowing smile on her lips, Geraldine reached out a hand and tweaked his tie, ostensibly straightening it in a playful manner, but using the gesture to draw even nearer to his tall frame.

Robbie didn't smile in response, but he didn't pull back either. He kept talking, his voice pitched too low for Julia to catch.

Geraldine mock pouted, but then quick as a flash, she laughed merrily and whirled away from him. By her manner she obviously expected him to follow, and he did.

The script in Julia's hand gave a slight wheeze of protest, and she realized she was gripping it too tightly. Relaxing her fingers, she turned. It was time to go. A dozen feet behind her, Harriet Vines stood in the shadows watching the exchange as well, a worried look on her face. She didn't seem to even notice Julia as she passed. As unobtrusively as she could, Julia slipped away from the clubhouse and out into the open air of the evening. The cool breeze made her realize that her cheeks were flushed. Which was silly. Of course, Geraldine was flirting with Robbie, and of course, he was responding to her. It was absolutely ridiculous to feel any sort of surprise.

Julia gloried in the exercise of the walk, taking longer strides than she might have normally. She needed to get home and check on Pop. She'd practically been ignoring him lately, because she was all caught up in the play. But she'd be headed back to school soon, and she'd miss him like anything. Feeling as if she were rousing from some sort of dream, Julia slid the rolled-up play in her skirt pocket. The play wasn't very important. It was time she got her head out of the clouds and back to real life. The Park was an illusion. A dream. She would never, could never, belong there and she had no business acting as if she could.

The next day, Pop finally lifted his prohibition against her working and Julia spent the morning at the shop. Unable to sit still or concentrate on anything meaningful, she flung herself into a series of the sort of odd jobs that usually tended to get left until an indefinite "later." Tidying the office and filing receipts and invoices, she was able to submerge her anxiety beneath superficial concentration.

Pop looked in on her a few times, a quizzical look on his face. Normally she avoided these tasks like the plague. But he had given up trying to make her go home and rest. Her feverish concentration had her finished with everything she could think of far too soon. She cast about for something else to do, thoughts buzzing too close and loud in her ears if she gave them any space.

Out in the shop she was relieved to find that the large plate glass windows were smudged and needed washing. A bucket of hot soapy water later she wound a kerchief around her hair and covered her tidy shirtwaist in an enormous old smock apron.

Heedless of the customers trickling in and out of

the shop she perched on a footstool and attacked the smudges with a vengeance, standing on tiptoe and reaching as high as she could. The tinkle of the bell over the door was followed by a cloud of expensively sweet perfume. She paid no attention, until a drawling voice addressed her.

"Julia, that's quite the charming ensemble. Don't you think so, Harriet?"

Julia stiffened and turned, careful to keep her expression nonchalant. Geraldine Scott and Harriet Vines stood looking up at her. "Are you trying to start a new fashion? I'm not sure 'drudge' is a style likely to catch on."

Geraldine's smirk made Julia want to smack her. Instead she carefully refrained from fidgeting with her apron or kerchief. "Hello Geraldine, Harriet. To what do we owe the honor?"

"Oh, we came to see you. Doesn't your father own this place? Isn't there someone else who can do that?"

"I consider it a character building exercise."

Geraldine stood rooted, looking at her expectantly while Harriet's gaze roved the room. It was obvious that they had come for some purpose and they weren't going anywhere until they had accomplished that purpose. Whatever it was.

Julia stepped down from the ladder. Her mother's training prodded her. "Can I get you something?"

"I remember you used to make a pleasant orange cream soda."

Julia nodded. "Anything for you, Harriet?"

"No, thank you." She pursed her mouth in a prim line.

Julia walked behind the long counter and went about

making Geraldine's soda. She considered adding a little something…extra to the frosty glass, but stopped herself at the last moment. She had just given Robbie that lecture about the Golden Rule after all. And besides, she was better than that. She would not be petty.

She stuck a striped straw into the soda then carried it and a glass of water over to the table the Parkies had claimed, and sat down with them.

Geraldine took a long sip then set the glass aside. "Delicious." She smiled as if she were bestowing an enormous favor. "Working in a quaint little shop like this really is your calling I think. I can just see you and some nice village boy settling down and running this shop together after your father passes." Her slender fingers swirled the straw around in the glass.

Julia regretted her earlier restraint. "Was there something specific you wanted to talk about?"

Harriet took an abstemious little sip from her water, making a face all the while.

Geraldine gave a half laugh. "It's just—" she fluttered her hands "—we're concerned for you."

Julia's heart beat faster. Did they know something about the fire? "Yes?"

Geraldine glanced around the shop. "It's Robbie Malcolm."

Julia sat back. "Robbie?" Why would Robbie have burned a copy of the script? Putting on the play had been his idea. It made no sense. Then the other shoe dropped and she knew what they were up to.

Harriet nodded sadly. Pushing away her glass of water as if it were a temptation she could not trust herself to have too near.

Geraldine shrugged her delicate shoulders, and shook

her head. "We wanted to make sure that he wasn't giving you ideas. He…he can sometimes be a bit too free with the Townies. Nothing really improper of course, but he's so charming and considerate the girls begin to think he means more by it than he really does."

Julia crossed her arms across her chest and bit the inside of her cheek to keep from laughing. "Oh really? Do tell me more."

Geraldine took another long draw on her orange soda. "You've been so kind to allow us to use your play and to come help direct things. We would hate to see you get hurt—you know, when the play is over and you aren't coming into the Park any longer, and he forgets about you."

Julia glanced from Geraldine to Harriet, who sat with her hands clasped, staring at the marble top of the small table.

"That is very compassionate of you." Julia let her hands rest lightly in her lap. She had finally realized that Geraldine's dislike was more than mere snobbery. She was jealous. Geraldine's name had been loosely linked with Robbie Malcolm's for years. Only he never had actually proposed. Geraldine wasn't really a debutante anymore. She must be wondering why it was taking him so long. And she definitely would not appreciate it if she thought he was showing interest in someone else.

Geraldine said something else, looking to Harriet for agreement. Julia didn't hear. If they only knew how much she had been avoiding even the thought of Robbie Malcolm all morning, they wouldn't have bothered to come.

"I do appreciate your warning. It's…kind of you to come and educate me about the situation."

"Does this mean you'll stop leading Robbie on?" Harriet asked.

Julia raised an eyebrow and stared at the other girl. "Excuse me?"

An unbecoming, splotchy red flush crept up Harriet's neck and into her cheeks.

Geraldine scowled. "Oh, don't mind Harriet, she didn't mean it liked it sounded."

Julia stood. She'd had about enough of both of them. She might easily have reassured them that she had absolutely no interest in Robbie Malcolm, but she just couldn't bring herself to do it. Her feelings or lack thereof were none of their business. "I will be sure to speak to Robbie about your concerns and I will ask him to clarify his intentions. But for now, as you can see I was quite busy, and the afternoon rush will be starting soon." She turned away, then turned back to them. "But do feel free to stay and finish your drinks."

She turned her back on them and crossed to the front of the store where she resumed her place on the stepladder. A moment later the bell over the door jangled and she saw them both marching away from the ice cream parlor. Geraldine's ladylike languor had been replaced with martial, manlike strides, while Harriet bobbed along after her, half trotting, half running to keep pace.

It should have been funny, but about the only thing Julia felt at the moment was queasy. She scrubbed furiously at the glass. She couldn't hold a candle to Geraldine's fortune and sophistication, but for some reason the other girl considered her a threat. And for her part, Julia didn't mind that one whit. She would show them that village girls were worth as much as Parkie girls, and maybe more.

In a flash it occurred to Julia that she had approached the problem of the fire all wrong. She shouldn't have been asking Parkies for information about themselves. She should have gone straight to the people she knew and trusted and who trusted her. The people who knew all about the Parkies anyway, and might be willing to share.

The Townies.

"Julia." Her father's voice smashed her reverie. "You're gonna rub clean through that window."

Startled, Julia jerked and dropped her cloth into the bucket of sudsy water, sending up a mini geyser.

"Sorry, Pop."

He shook his head in his eternally bewildered, fatherly way, and retreated back behind the counter.

Julia cleaned up the spilled water and went to pour out the wastewater in the garden patch behind the parlor. She needed to talk to Minna and the other girls. Almost all of her friends worked as maids of one kind or another up at the Park. They would be able to tell her something. All she had to do was ask.

Robbie stared out the window at the spreading, manicured lawns of the club grounds as Tommy Beyers rambled on and on about his plans to win the upcoming regatta. Was getting answers about Friedrich really worth this torture? The fellow was so boring.

Robbie toyed with the fork in his hand. He just had to let the man talk until he could steer the conversation in the right direction. It had taken him all morning to find out which of the great houses Friedrich worked for. And now that he'd come this far he wasn't going to let the effort go to waste.

When he could at last take it no longer, he interrupted the outpouring. "I understand you have a new auto."

"Oh, yes." Good-natured and oblivious, Tommy happily started down a new avenue of self-congratulations. "She's a beauty all right. As spiffy as your little ride, I'll bet."

Robbie had to bite his tongue to keep from issuing a challenge then and there. He could drive circles around Tommy Beyers with his eyes crossed and a pumpkin to steer with. Holding his competitive instincts in check, he said, "Oh, you're driving it yourself? I thought your family had a chauffeur."

"We do all right. But that's for the family rig. They're so pedestrian, they can't stand the least bit of real speed."

"Must be an older fellow then, no young buck wants to hold too tight on the throttle."

"No, Friedrich's about our age, I'd say. He's actually a ripping good driver if they let him off the reins a bit. If he was a Parkie I'd challenge him to a race to test his mettle."

"Has he been there long? I thought your pater had some doddering old soul?"

"Oh, he's been around awhile I guess. Used to be a groom I think, but he's all for anything new. Calls it progress." He said this in the manner of someone relating the interests of a child. "When father first thought of getting a car, he consulted me of course, and then he talked to Friedrich. The fellow knew all there was to know about autos, and told the old man just what to get."

"He sounds knowledgeable."

Tommy shrugged. "I guess. But how did we ever get on the subject of the help?"

Robbie laughed and took a swig from his glass. "You brought it up I think. But since you did, my old man is thinking about getting an auto for him and mother. Father would probably be okay, but I think mother would need some kind of driver."

"Ha! Now I'm onto you, you sly old dog! Servant poaching. The oldest and most popular sport at the Park."

Robbie held up his hands in mock surrender. "The thought crossed my mind, but it sounds like there might be some likely lad hanging about our place already."

The idea that the Beyer success with their groom could be duplicated seemed to bring out the competitor in Tommy. He shook his head. "I don't think so. Friedrich is one of a kind. Quite intelligent actually. Not something you expect from a groom."

"How did you discover this gem among grooms?"

"Caught him reading actually. He tried to hide the book, but I had him hand it over. A book called *What is Property.* Rather simplistic." Tommy chuckled. "But I thought it spoke well of his desire to better himself."

Glass half way to his mouth, Robbie blinked at him. "*What is Property?* You're sure?"

Derailed in his tale, Tommy blinked owlishly. "I think so."

"I'm sorry. Do go on."

Tommy did. Droning on and on, having managed to turn a conversation about Friedrich into accolades for himself. Robbie listened with only one ear. If Tommy knew what he was praising his groom for reading…

He was fairly certain that the author's answer to his title's question was—"Property is theft." Friedrich was reading anarchist literature right in the heart of the Park.

If Tommy had had any idea what Friedrich's book had really been about he'd have sacked him on the spot. And no doubt Friedrich was laughing up his sleeve at the poor sap the entire time he was being congratulated on his diligence.

The fellow was bolder and trickier than Robbie had first credited. He glanced down and realized too late that he had bent the spoon in his hand. He tried to straighten it out then placed it gently in his uneaten bowl of soup. All he could think of was Julia's outraged expression when he had suggested that Friedrich might have been involved in either of the incidents at the Park. The poor girl was so blinded by his handsome face that she couldn't see that he could pose a threat. That meant it was up to Robbie to keep her safe and thwart whatever Friedrich might be planning. The fire might just have been the beginning.

Robbie opened his mouth to tell Tommy about his chauffeur, but decided against it. It was still possible the fellow wasn't guilty, and if he was innocent, then his whole life might be ruined if Robbie spoke out of turn. Julia would never forgive him. She had made a valid point earlier, too. It didn't make much sense for the script to have been burned on Julia's porch. Friedrich had been there when Robbie had coerced Julia into allowing them to put on her play. So why not burn it on Robbie's porch? Unless he viewed Julia's agreement as some sort of personal betrayal. The thought made him break out in a cold sweat. It smacked of an unhealthy sort of obsession.

Besides, if he exposed the fellow and Friedrich was sacked, they might never know if he planned something more, something bigger, in time to stop him. Anarchists around the world had been growing more and more violent. This could just be the beginning of Friedrich's campaign against the Park. And what if it wasn't just Friedrich's campaign? Robbie's stomach gave a little lurch. What if he was part of a group? What if there were more anarchists in the Park?

Robbie had to get to the bottom of all this and he had to do it quickly.

Chapter 10

Julia itched for Thursday afternoon. Minna's afternoon off meant she would come into the village to see her family, and she always stopped in at the ice cream parlor for a treat. But this time, Julia had more in mind than a casual chat.

Every time the bell chimed, Julia's head popped up. Unfortunately that meant she caught Robbie's eye the moment he walked in the door.

He smiled when he saw her, and he looked so glad that she couldn't help thawing a little.

Just as he had the last time, he took a stool at the long counter. But this time he carried an extravagantly wrapped box in his arms.

She needed to remember that they weren't friends. If she treated him like any other customer, everything would be fine. "What would you like today, Mr. Malcolm?"

He winced. "Mr. Malcolm is it? You know how to fillet a fellow, don't you?"

"Me?" Julia's pretense of distance evaporated. "You're the one who made it quite clear that we are of different stations. I'm only trying to remember my place."

"Miss Wren, you know quite well that I didn't mean anything of the sort. Now how about you tell me why you walked home the other evening? I was worried about you. I had to follow and make sure you got home safe, so I might as well have had the pleasure of your company."

Julia had known he was following. It wasn't as if that Mercedes of his was subtle, even though he'd kept his distance. It had been kind of sweet. She wasn't prepared to let him off the hook that easily however. "I'm afraid that is a pleasure you'll have to forego."

"I made a promise to your father, and I intend to keep it."

She shook her head. "I've been warned away from you."

"Warned away? Did someone threaten you?" He stood. "Was there another fire or something worse?" His eyes held a glint of mayhem. His fists clenched and unclenched. He looked as if he was about to dart out into the street and start a fight with someone. Proba-bly Friedrich, the way he had been talking about him.

"No. It was ostensibly a very pleasant call by Ger-aldine and Harriet." She smiled as she slapped down an ice cream sundae in front of him. "They are quite concerned that I might make a fool of myself over you, and by their report I wouldn't be the first."

"You?" He sounded grumpy as he spooned up a bite

of creamy vanilla ice cream and chocolate syrup. "It's much more likely that I'll be the one to look foolish."

Eyebrow cocked, Julia grabbed a damp towel and began wiping down the already immaculate counter. "That's what I thought."

He grinned and ate another bite of his sundae, his good humor reestablishing itself. "I hope you don't pay them any mind. I never do."

"No?"

"No." He emphasized his point by stabbing his spoon into the ice cream.

"But I understood that you and Geraldine are very nearly engaged."

He shook his head. "That's what my parents want. Hers too I think." He licked his spoon. "No one bothered to consult us, of course."

"Are you sure?" Julia set down the towel and looked at him. "I got the impression that Geraldine wouldn't mind. In fact, I think she's rather counting on it."

"She has every other man in the Park catering to her whims. I think she can do without me."

"Perhaps that's why she can't." Julia raised her eyebrows and glided away.

Abandoning his sundae, he followed. "That's not fair. I've never been anything but friendly to Geraldine."

Julia shrugged. "I'm not arguing the point. I just think she may have a different perception of the situation." She stopped and turned back to him. "Can you think of any reason she might have that impression?"

The tips of his ears turned magenta and the fire was back in his eyes.

"That's what I thought." She turned away and retreated to the office. She closed the door and then sat down in Pop's chair. Elbows on the desk she let her head rest against her balled fists.

That was an end to it. She'd give him time to leave before she went back out to the shop. It was a pretty good bet that he wouldn't expect her to show up for the practice. Almost all the scene action had been sorted so that people knew where they were supposed to be. Robbie had really handled it all anyway. She was director in name only. There was no reason she had to be present for the play.

The door opened.

Julia whipped her head up. "Don't worry, Po—"

Robbie stood in the doorway. Moving into the small space and making it feel much smaller, he shut the door behind him. "You're not worried about Geraldine. Everyone knows she can take care of herself. What was that really about?"

Julia stood to face him. "I did not invite you to follow me."

Robbie scowled. "Cards on the table time, Miss Wren. I've never cared a hang for Geraldine, but I can't say the same about you."

She clasped her hands together to hide their trembling and scowled right back. "Don't talk rubbish."

"I'm not." His gaze was hot enough to singe.

"No? Well perhaps you mean it when you say it, but your reputation precedes you. How many times have you said such a thing to someone like me? A girl who doesn't count."

He retreated as if she had punched him in the chest and driven the breath from him. Then he crossed the length of the room in two strides and grabbed her hand.

"Never to someone like you. I've never met anyone like you."

She tried to pull her hand free, but he held on, and raised it to his lips. She stopped struggling and he kissed the back of her hand gently.

His hands moved up her arms to take her by the shoulders. He held her there. Not hurting her, but not freeing her either, while his eyes searched her face. Abruptly he released her. "But I can see I have work to do."

He whirled away and strode out the door, then popped his head back around the frame. "I shall pick you up at six, as usual. Don't walk again."

And then he was gone.

That was the second time he'd kissed her hand. And against all common sense, she had wanted him to be the slightest bit less respectful and kiss her properly.

Julia dropped back into the chair. Her knees were wobbly and her hand tingled and her heart raced. Love didn't seem to agree with her. At the moment it resembled nothing so much as the flu.

What was she thinking? This wasn't love. It couldn't be. It was only attraction—infatuation maybe. But not love. She didn't know Robbie well enough for that. And aside from that, there was no future for them either way. His family would never stand for such a union, and she would never stand for anything less. Best to close the door of her heart to any such ideas.

A shadow filled the door and Julia blinked, trying to refocus.

"Are you all right?" Minna's voice was sweet and worried.

"Minna, you're here! I'm so glad. I've been aching to talk to you."

Minna's eyebrows rose. "I've missed you, too."

Julia led her back into the parlor to fix her a malted.

Robbie's parcel was still on the counter. He must have forgotten it. Julia studiously tried to ignore it. But Minna claimed a seat next to it. "Looks like someone forgot their package." She checked the tag. Her eyebrow rose. "It's for you."

"Me?" Julia spilled the malt powder.

"So long as you're Julia."

Julia finished making Minna's malted, then took the package from her and looked around. Gingerly, as if she expected it to explode, she tweaked open the card.

In small neat print it read, "For Julia. In case of emergency."

"Go ahead and open it." Minna took a long swig of her drink.

Wishing she had privacy, but knowing Minna would never let her demur, Julia teased open the green satin bow that bound the B. Altman's package closed. She lifted the lid off and smoothed back several layers of crisp tissue paper until she laid bare several bulbous glass shapes.

"What are they?" Minna leaned over the counter to the lower work area where Julia had placed the box.

Julia pulled one out and held it up. Clear liquid sloshed about inside. "We have these at Barnard. They're fire grenades."

"What?"

Julia grinned at Minna. "You throw them at a fire to extinguish it."

Minna frowned in response. "Because of your porch fire?"

"I think so."

"But why? Is someone mocking you?"

Julia shook her head. "I think he's trying to be sweet."

Minna looked at her askance. "Who is? Is this from Mr. Malcolm?" She leaned forward, her voice a horrified whisper. "He was in the office with you. You shouldn't be alone with him and you should not be getting gifts from a Parkie. This does not look good. What will your father say?"

She should have just refused to open the box. "It is hardly something objectionable." Julia waggled the glass bulb at Minna, then placed it gently back in its tissue-swathed berth. "It's the sort of gesture any concerned friend might make."

Minna snorted. "Do not put on your stubborn face with me. I know you too well. I thought you were too smart to get involved with a Parkie."

"I'm not involved with him."

Julia was saved from an argument by the arrival of a party of half a dozen Parkie youngsters. She was busy for several minutes preparing treats to stringent specifications imposed by the customers who had very decided notions about their preferences.

She came back to Minna determined to get the conversation on the track she had originally intended. "Have you had any trouble because of our picnic in the Park?"

Minna slurped up the last of her chocolate malt. "No. Not a bit. Although I've caught Harriet staring at me from time to time like she's thinking hard about something."

"But she hasn't threatened you or anything?"

Minna shook her head. "If anything she's been nicer than usual. She actually seemed to like your play and she asked me several questions about you."

"About me?"

"Don't worry." Minna stuck out a hand. "She didn't pry. I wouldn't have told her anything private."

"But what sorts of things was she asking?"

"Oh, about Barnard, and when you'd be going back. Whether you had a beau. Those sorts of things. Nothing too personal, I promise."

Julia nodded. That made sense. Since Harriet knew Julia and Minna were friends she must have been trying to gather information for Geraldine. They would naturally want to gauge how much of a threat she might be.

Julia glanced quickly around. No one was paying them any mind. "So, about the fire."

"Yes." Minna shoved aside her empty glass. "What happened?"

Julia leaned in even closer. "It was a script."

Minna frowned. "What was a script?"

"The—what was used to start the fire on the porch. Someone burned a copy of the script from my play."

Minna gasped, a hand to her mouth. "Did you tell the police?"

"The police never even came out." Julia shook her head. "The firemen decided right away that it was some sort of prank that got out of hand."

"What do you think?"

"I think it was someone who doesn't want a Townie's play put on at the Park."

"But surely not. That seems so petty. And there are already too many people involved in making the play happen. Would they even have time to work up something different at this point?"

Minna had a point. Julia persisted. "Maybe they'd rather not have a play at all than put on mine."

Minna shook her head. "The Parkies can be stuck up, but I don't know any that are insane. Why would they care about your play that much? They'll do a different one next year, and a different one the year after that. Even if they were annoyed would they care that much?"

"I don't know. But Parkies are the only ones who had copies of the script." She ought to have thought of it before. "Do you think we could get all the girls to look for the scripts?"

"What are you talking about?"

"Don't you see? Whoever doesn't have their script could be the one who set the fire."

"But what girls?"

"You, Peggy, Marie, Giada, everyone."

"Are you telling me that you want your friends to spy for you? They could lose their jobs. *We* could lose our jobs."

"I don't want anyone to lose their jobs. But they're maids after all. They clean up after people. Surely it's not unusual for them to see things lying around." Julia shrugged and picked up a cloth and scrubbed the counter.

"It's not that simple, Julia. Take Giada, she's a scullery maid. She's not allowed upstairs except to deliver the coal. And besides that, she can't read, at least not English. And neither can most of the other girls."

"I could show them what the cover looks like."

"No." Minna's voice was slightly raised and after a glance around she lowered it. "You are not going to drag our friends into this. You're talking about their livelihoods. That may not mean much to you with your father's prosperous business to rely upon, but we need our jobs. We cannot be out of work."

Julia didn't flinch, but Minna's words stung. Apparently she wasn't really considered a Townie either. "Then what do I do? Wait to be burned out of my house?"

"None of this would have even started except that you just had to picnic in the park."

Julia's cheeks tingled like she'd been slapped. "I'm doing everything I can to make sure that doesn't cause problems for you. I never meant for any of this to happen."

"You never do. But your grand ideas could get someone fired or worse."

Julia slapped down the cloth. "What do you mean by that?"

Minna shook her head. "Most of the families are fine to work for, and usually the work is light because they're not in residence year-round."

"But?"

Minna sighed. "But there are one or two who aren't so nice at all. They could make life miserable for a girl even if they didn't fire her."

"What do you mean?"

Minna glanced around, then got up and dragged Julia out back. Even then her voice lowered into little more than a whisper. "All right. You want to know what some of them are like?" She shook her head. "One of our friends told me that her employer's daughter throws terrible tantrums if she doesn't get her way. Not just stomping her feet and shouting. She flies into a rage. She didn't like a dress that had been ordered for her, a beautiful ball gown from Mrs. Donovan in New York, and you know how expensive those are."

Julia nodded.

"Well when it arrived it wasn't exactly the way she wanted, she took scissors to it and shredded it. There was nothing left but a pile of rags when she was done."

Shocked, Julia's mouth hung open. "But don't her parents do anything?"

"She has them both cowed and they don't dare murmur a peep. After that fit, they ordered her a new dress and everyone went about their business like normal, 'cept for our friend who had to clean up the mess."

A rage like that—a rage a family managed to keep hidden from the world at large—that could be the sign of someone who was unstable enough to threaten someone they perceived as thwarting them.

Julia opened her mouth.

Minna held up her hand. "Don't even ask who it was. I'm not telling you. You'll badger the maid until she tells you things or does something for you, and ends up getting sacked for her trouble."

Julia needed to find out more, but it looked like she'd have to do it without Minna's help.

Chapter 11

The next morning, Robbie drove into the city like a tiger was on his tail. The wind felt wonderful, kind of cleansing. He pushed the car to the limits of what it could do. At one point he passed a police officer along the road, but the fellow could do no more than shake a fist and swear. The police were going to have to get cars of their own if they wanted to keep pace with progress.

Reluctantly he parked in Weehawken. He walked to the ferry office, and plunked down his money for passage. They really needed to build a bridge that would link the rest of the civilized world to Manhattan. He would much rather be racing along at his own speed, rather than plodding at the pace of a ferry.

On another day he might have been delighted at his timing, but today, the twenty minutes he had to wait for the ferry to cast off were interminable. He prowled the decks, pacing off his unease, as if his measured tread might encourage the ship to go faster.

His conversation with Julia had gone all wrong. He had wanted to warn her about Friedrich and tell her what he had discovered. He'd known that she wouldn't be happy with the news and had armed himself with gifts, but she'd still managed to catch him off guard.

He'd reacted badly. He should have kept his fool mouth shut. That seemed to be a recurring theme for him. He hadn't even gotten around to bringing Friedrich up in the conversation.

Worst of all, she had been right. He had allowed the easy assumptions of his parents and friends to color his behavior toward Geraldine. If he was honest he too had assumed that they would end up married in some hazy, far distant future. But it had all been very amorphous, just like everything else in his future.

It was time—past time really—that he decide. Really decide, not drift along with the current of events, but determine what he wanted in life, and what he was willing to do to get it.

He had some thinking to do.

But first he needed to learn more about Friedrich Bauer and figure out whether the fellow was a threat.

The great ferry pulled into the dock on the other side of the river and Robbie was the first in line to disembark. Normally he wouldn't have minded getting in line. But today he was on a mission. He didn't have the patience to wait on little old ladies and wailing toddlers.

He had already talked to the police in Tuxedo. Since he didn't want to harm Friedrich's reputation without cause, however, he hadn't learned much. Just that there

had never been any complaints about him at the Park.
Nor did he have any criminal record so far as they were
aware.

The gangplank was hardly in place before Robbie
was striding across it and up to the bank of cabbies.
With a flick of a coin he hired the first in the row. "To
city hall."

The driver had caught the coin with a deft grab. He
touched the brim of his cap. "Sure thing."

Robbie jumped inside. He needed to know more.
Much more. And the best place to find it was in New
York. One of his friends was an assistant district at-
torney and he knew there had been ongoing investigations into the anarchist groups that dotted the city like
smallpox boils. If Friedrich was a part of any of those
groups, Eddie would know about it.

At city hall, Robbie bounded up the curving main
staircase, passing flunkies and functionaries of all
kinds. Heads turned and disapproving glares followed
his swift passage. He sneered back. He had important
things to do. They were small men with puny imagina-
tions and dull dreams. They didn't matter.

He nearly tripped on the last step, at the thought of
what Julia would have had to say to that sentiment.
Wasn't that what she'd been trying to tell him? He
slowed his pace. He thought of himself as enlightened
because he was polite, even considerate to those he considered less. But the mere fact that he considered them
less than himself was the issue. That was the basis for
all her objections. Because what was *he* after all? A
sponge who lived off his father's money and put nothing back into society. What right did he have to sneer
at anyone?

He looked more closely into the faces of the men he passed. Some had furrowed, worried brows. A few smiled and nodded when he met their gaze. Others were involved in animated discussions and didn't so much as glance in his direction. Every one of them had a past, had a story. And more than that, they had value in God's eyes. Just as much value as he or any Parkie. How could he presume to tell their stories through pictures if he couldn't truly see them?

Preoccupied, he pushed open the door into Eddie's office. His path was immediately impeded by not one, but three clerks. These worthies looked up from their typewriters and surveyed him with disinterest as he entered.

The fellow in the back spoke up first. "Yes?"

Under his fish-eyed glare, Robbie slipped off his hat. "I'm here to see Eddie Randolph."

"Mr. Randolph?"

How many Eddie Randolphs worked in the place? "Yes."

The response was immediate. "I'm afraid he isn't available at the moment."

"Is he over at the courthouse?"

"No. He's here, but he can't be disturbed."

Robbie unpacked his most charming smile. "We're old friends. I think he'd be willing to make an exception."

The flunky's smile was thin lipped. "We don't make exceptions. Rules are in place for a reason."

Even ten minutes ago, Robbie would have narrowed his eyes and rolled right over this popinjay. But he took a moment to look more closely. The fellow's eyes had dark circles beneath them, and a worried V spiking between them. His manner and appearance were fastidious aside from a slight trembling in his hands. In short he looked like the sort of man who always tried to do the proper thing. And yet this man who likely prided himself on being unflappable appeared to be under great stress.

Robbie modulated his tone. "When would be a better time to see him?"

The fellow glanced over his shoulder at the door set squarely in the back wall. "I suppose I could—"

At that moment the door opened and Robbie was delivered from clerical purgatory when Eddie himself stepped out.

"Well hello, you old goat." Eddie strode forward and clasped his hand. "I never looked for you today!"

"I happened to be in town, and I thought I'd come see you."

"You took a break from flirting with pretty girls and joyriding in that auto of yours, to unearth me in this old mausoleum?" He planted his hands on his hips. A glint of humor shone in his eye. "I may not be as young as you, and I'm burdened by family cares, but I'm not in my dotage yet. Out with it. What is it you want?"

Robbie glanced around at the studiously busy clerks. "How about I tell you over lunch."

Eddie fixed him with a glare. "You're paying."

"I wouldn't have it any other way."

"In that case, let me grab my jacket." He nipped back to the inner office and came back out with his suit jacket on.

A moment later they were turning into a café around the corner from city hall. The place was overflowing with office workers snatching a quick noonday meal.

Redolent of coffee, haste and the scent of cooking meat, the pace inside was pitched just under frantic.

With the skill of long practice, Eddie snagged a table for them by the window as the former occupants rose. "You've got to try the pot roast."

"Pot roast?"

Eddie nodded. "Pot roast."

A woman in a much-stained apron took their order for pot roast and darted away.

"Now spill. What is it you're after?"

"I was wondering what you could tell me about the anarchists in New York."

Eddie's eyebrows rose. "Anarchists? Surely you haven't taken up a new hobby?"

Robbie snorted and plucked at the lapels of his superbly tailored jacket. "Somehow I don't think they'd have me."

"You might be surprised."

The waitress all but flew up to their table and plopped down two plates piled high with mashed potatoes that had been topped by pot roast and vegetables and liberally doused with dark, rich gravy.

Robbie inhaled, and suddenly he was ravenous. "This doesn't look like—"

"Eat it."

Robbie complied. With the first bite he forgot what they'd been talking about and why they were here.

Luckily, Eddie hadn't forgotten. He launched into a diatribe about the trouble anarchists had been causing in the city, punctuated only when he stopped to eat a bite. He didn't slow until he'd scooped the last bit of mashed potatoes. He grinned ruefully. "I think you may have gotten more than you bargained for."

Robbie grinned back. "It was every bit as enthralling as one of Professor Grundy's best lessons."

Eddie chucked his remaining crust of bread at Robbie's head. "And I know how highly you thought of old Grumpy Grundy." Then he sobered and shook his head. "The thing is the anarchists have changed. For years they were little more than a social club for the disgruntled, but now…" He shook his head. "Now they are spreading. And they are dangerous. More hostile." His brows drew together. "I'm afraid it's only a matter of time before they erupt in violence."

Robbie swallowed a bite that had suddenly gone dry. "What do we do?"

Eddie shrugged. "We keep an eye on them. Figure out who the leaders are. Try to stay a step ahead of them. Stop them before they can enact something."

"So you have men in their groups?"

"A few. It's not easy for them to maintain a facade indefinitely."

Robbie leaned closer. "I have a dilemma. There's a man working at the Park. I have reason to believe that he could be involved with the anarchists, but I don't want to ruin his reputation, his job and his life unless there's no doubt. But I can't sit back and do nothing. There have been a few…incidents."

"What kind of incidents?"

Robbie described the reasons for his concern.

When he finished Eddie wiped his mouth with his napkin and was quiet for a long moment. It took all Robbie's restraint not to demand a response. But he knew from experience that the best way to get Eddie to talk was to let him think through all the angles first. Rushing him along didn't accomplish a thing.

"Who's the man?" he asked at last.

"His name is Friedrich Bauer. But all I have is suspicion. No proof of anything."

Eddie nodded thoughtfully. "We have reports on most everyone who is part of the anarchist groups. If he's an anarchist we'll find out." He pushed away from the table and stood.

Back at city hall, Eddie had one of his lackeys start pulling records. He invited Robbie into his office to wait.

Robbie rubbed his palms on his pants. Suddenly awkward, and not sure at all that he was doing the right thing. What would he do if Friedrich wasn't an anarchist? What would he do if he was? Inwardly he prayed for guidance. Then he cast about for a topic of conversation that didn't involve plots and mayhem. "How are Lillian and the girls?"

"Pining for Tuxedo Park. We haven't made it out all summer. I've been too busy here at work, and she won't leave without me."

"So runs the course of true love."

Eddie grinned. "I have to admit I'm not complaining. I'd miss my girls like fury if they ran off all week without me."

Robbie smiled, envy bittersweet in the back of his throat. "You're a lucky man."

"A blessed man," Eddie corrected. He shook his head. "Five years ago I never would have thought I'd be where I am."

"What do you mean?"

"I know you were away at school during that time, but you must have heard. My dad was furious when he heard I wanted to go into public office rather than join the family firm. And of course Mother didn't much care for the idea of me marrying Lillian because she considered her *nouveau riche*.

"I was a mess until I buckled down and got myself sorted out. I started going to church. I decided that if I was going to be my own man I had to act like it, so I got a job with the D.A.'s office and moved into an apartment. Then I started courting Lillian for real."

"But I've seen your parents with Lillian and the girls. They positively dote on them."

"They do now." Eddie grinned. "But for the first three years we didn't have much contact. I prayed every day. When Ava was born they began calling, and it wasn't long before they fell in love with Lillian, too." He pushed out a big puff of air and leaned back in his chair. "But that's enough about me. What adventures have you been up to?"

"Wait. How did you know it was the right decision?"

"To court Lillian, or to go to work for the D.A.?"

"Both."

Eddie shrugged. "I prayed about it. I put it all out there, and like the psalmist, asked God to order my steps. I felt at peace with the decision and moved forward."

"You weren't worried at all? What if your parents had been right about Lillian?"

"God knew Lillian. He wasn't going to steer me wrong. My parents, though, had never met her and were laboring under their prejudices. But you know—" he leaned back in his chair "—before I reached a place of peace, I had to get to the point where I was willing to give her up if that was what God wanted. That was the hardest thing I've ever done. But it wasn't until I finally put Him first things began to click into place."

Robbie tried to absorb this. How could anyone trust the unseen so completely? Was it really God leading him or had Eddie lucked out?

A knock sounded at the door. A brilliantined fellow stepped in carrying a slim manila folder. "I believe this is the file you wished to see."

Eddie accepted it and flipped it open. The assistant withdrew, a curious glance flickering over Robbie as he left.

"Not much here, I'm afraid." Eddie flipped it around and slid it across to Robbie who reached for it eagerly.

The file contained only three pages. They detailed Friedrich's attendance at a handful of meetings of The Brotherhood of Man. The last meeting he attended had been nearly a year previous. The file confirmed that he had no criminal history. He had been born in the United States to Austro-Hungarian immigrants. His father was now deceased. His mother ill. He had a single sister. Based on the file it seemed that he had done nothing more than dabble. He wasn't known to be any sort of leader or even a regular participant.

"What of this group, 'The Brotherhood of Man'?"

Eddie rolled his eyes. "Am I the only one who finds anarchists the most pretentious collection of humanity around?"

"With the exception of Tuxedo Park of course." Robbie grinned.

Eddie snorted, "Yes. With that possible exception. The Brotherhood of Man isn't one of the groups with known radical tendencies. They are philosophers, daydreamers, layabouts and absinthe-addled muckrakers. But from what I know they are not violent."

Robbie stared down at the few pages in his hands. "How much would it take to push one of them to violence?"

Eddie raised his hands. "Only God can see into the heart. All I can tell you is that they've never caused any problems."

A few minutes later, Robbie took his leave. He hailed a cab, and began reversing the process that had brought him into the city. He'd managed to confirm that Friedrich had anarchist leanings, but hadn't managed to rule him in or out when it came to the problems at the Park.

What did that leave him with?

His frantic energy had deserted him, and he slumped on one of the ferry benches. It was a relief to finally climb back behind the wheel of his car. The green gloom of the Ramapo Mountains soon swallowed him up. It was restful following the winding road, and at last he released the problem he'd been clutching at. As dusk fell, he took an abrupt turn onto a side road, driving up the mountain until he overlooked Tuxedo village. The thin silver sliver of the river, the train station, the neat little post office and amputated row of shops. They looked fairytale pristine in the last light of the dying day.

He'd been avoiding it. Rebelling against it for a year now, but there was nothing for it. He had to make up his mind. He couldn't continue on as he was, which left him with two options. He could either embrace his father's agenda, i.e. woo and marry Geraldine and settle down to a job in the family business, or he could strike out on his own to either succeed or fail. Doing that would probably mean giving up everything he was accustomed to. The ease and luxury would be the first to go. Could he handle it? What did he really want?

His conversation with Eddie echoed through his thoughts. And for the first time he considered not just his own desires, but what God wanted for him.

On the horizon, beyond the village, a smudgy shimmer of orange-red blossomed against the dark of the night. Robbie stared at it for a moment wondering what it could be. And then as if the alarm had reached him he knew.

It was fire.

Shoving his car into gear he turned and raced down the mountainside toward the Park.

Chapter 12

Julia pushed the flat of her hand into the stitch at her side as she drew close enough to see the flames. Greedily they licked at the sides of the shed. Tendrils hissed and turned the shingled cedar black. Who could have done this? And why? The only thing the shed held were the props and art supplies for the club's amateur theatricals.

She cast about for water. A pump with a bucket dangling from it stood by one of the gardening sheds and she raced to it.

Somewhere behind her there was a mounting uproar as servants and guests from the club poured out onto the grounds.

She pumped in a frenzy, a strange sense of déjà vu sluicing through her as the water splashed into the bucket. Bucket full at last, she dashed back to the shed and flung the water at the fire.

The flames reared back but then seemed to gather new strength, the cracking and popping of the wood became a roar as something inside ignited.

"Julia!"

She turned toward the voice. Robbie was arriving in his car, driving right across the lawn. He was flailing his arms and she moved toward him.

Then the hot arms of the fire seemed to reach out for her, snatching and roaring. Julia glanced back and as she did the shed exploded. She was tossed backward landing in the grass, her head reeling.

Bits of wood and nails pattered down on the grass all about her. A flurry of papier mâché swirled into the air as a brief shower of sparks shriveled to ash, floating back to earth in a grim parody of snow.

Robbie was beside her. Kneeling over her. "What were you thinking? There were all sorts of paint cans and turpentine in there. You might have been killed."

Dazed she just blinked at him.

Her ears seemed to be ringing. No. That wasn't right. As she gathered her wits the fire wagon arrived, its bell clanging mercilessly as it waded through spectators.

Robbie paid them no mind. He had hold of her shoulders and was yelling. "Julia!"

"Yes. Yes." She frowned and he stopped shaking her. "I'm all right."

"Oh, thank God." He slumped to the ground. "I thought you might have hit your head."

"I think I did a bit." She touched a tender spot on the back of her head. "But not too hard."

"What happened?"

She shook her head. "I don't know. We worked on some of the props this evening, and when we were done

Charlie and I put them in the shed. I started walking home. I got almost to the end of the drive, but then I looked back for some reason and saw the glow. I ran. I sounded the alarm, but by the time I got back, it was almost totally consumed. I only managed to get a single bucket of water on it."

Robbie put a gentle hand around her shoulders and pulled her close until her head nestled against his shoulder. "I was up on Fox Hill and saw the flames. I raced to get here."

She watched as the firefighters unloaded their hose on the flames. A sick feeling settled in her stomach. Her voice sounded hoarse to her own ears. "Robbie, I don't care anymore if it was a Parkie or a Townie, whoever has been doing these things has to be stopped."

He tightened his grip. "You're right. No more sides and no more silly games. We have to find out who is doing this and why."

Robbie removed his arm from around Julia as he became aware of speculative glances cast their way. He offered a hand, helping her to her feet. Then he forced himself to take a half step away, though he ached to keep an arm wrapped protectively around her shoulder.

The firefighters didn't take long to douse the flames, though in large part it seemed like the explosion had exhausted the blaze, leaving it weak and depleted.

Gil Bush the police chief wound his way through the crowd and Robbie wasn't surprised to see him ultimately head in their direction. The chief was a regular sight in the village. On the short side, but still trim. His white, walrus mustache could bristle with menace when he was perturbed which happened only when crime threatened the village, or when the Tuxedo team was in danger of losing a curling match.

"Evening, Miss Wren, I understand you was the first to arrive at the scene here."

Julia nodded. "Yes."

"So you were alone?"

Julia nodded slowly. "Yes."

The chief leaned in, examining her head to foot. "You're not hurt, are you?"

"Just shaken."

Robbie was quick to place a hand under her elbow. "Do you need to sit down?"

"No. I'm fine."

"Tell me what you saw, Miss Wren."

Julia repeated the story she had told Robbie earlier.

"You could have been hurt, why didn't you stay at the clubhouse once you raised the alarm?"

"I didn't know it was going to explode. I suppose I ought to have been more concerned about that. I knew there were paint cans in there. I wasn't thinking, I guess. Just…reacting."

The chief nodded. He stood with his thumbs hooked in his pants pockets, a casual stance. But his eyes were as attentive as Robbie had ever seen them. Something about the chief's watchfulness put Robbie on edge. He wanted to warn Julia to be careful. To guard her words. But the best he could do was squeeze her elbow before he released it.

She looked up at him questioningly.

"I understand that this shed was where the theatrical society keeps—kept—props and scenery and so on."

Robbie jumped in. "Yes, that's the case. There wasn't anything of much value in there."

"That's good to hear." The chief turned back to Julia, seemingly intent on conversing with her rather than Robbie. "And I hear the society is putting on a play you wrote."

Julia's nod was wary. *Good. Maybe she was starting to feel the strange way the chief was acting as well.*

"But you weren't too happy about that development, were you? Why is that? Seems like an honor to me."

"I wasn't happy at first," Julia admitted. "But when I figured out it wasn't some sort of elaborate joke… What?"

The chief's gaze was direct and piercing and Julia actually backed up a step. "I didn't set this fire."

Robbie stepped forward. "Sir, did you hear about the fire at Miss Wren's house? It's possible this could be related."

"How's that, young Malcolm?"

"Well someone—" He drew closer and lowered his voice, conscious of the people still milling about. "Someone set a fire on her front porch the other night."

The chief nodded gravely. "I was aware." He turned to Julia. "Why did you agree to let them put on your play?"

"I—that is. Well, Mr. Malcolm can be very persuasive."

"So I've heard." The chief cast Robbie an arch look.

"Sir, I'm afraid someone may actually be target—"

"Thank you for your assistance, Mr. Malcolm. I'll call on you if I need more information from you." He turned once more back to Julia. "Miss Wren, perhaps I could have a few more minutes of your time."

Robbie wasn't about to be dismissed. "Sir, I don't think you appreciate the gravity of the situation."

"No, son. I don't think you do. Arson's a serious offense."

"This was arson then?" Julia asked.

"Don't know yet. Things are pointing that way. There's a strong smell of turpentine for one thing. But I understand there was turpentine in the shed."

Julia nodded. "Yes. It was with the paint."

The chief's smile was as thin as his hair. "Miss Wren." He put his arm around her shoulder and drew her away from Robbie.

Julia glanced back over her shoulder, her eyes bewildered. Robbie followed right behind them. He had to strain to hear the chief. There was no way he was going to abandon Julia at this point though.

"I'm concerned for you, my dear."

"I'm fine. There's not much of a bump."

"Mmm hmm. I was thinking of something else."

She didn't respond.

"There is some concern among the residents that you might have been beguiled by the society here."

"Begui—?"

"Listen, my dear, it's understandable, your head is turned. You want to stay a part of the world here. To find ways to keep yourself interesting and retain the attention—"

She stopped dead. "Excuse me?"

"It's only to be expected that you'd be dazzled."

"How dare you?" She stood stiff and tall, the tips of her ears a brilliant pink. "I am not the one who set this fire. I didn't ask the Parkies to put on my play, and neither am I angling to set myself up as the pet Townie. I resent your implication and if you have nothing further,

I'm going home. I have a headache." She stalked away from him, her head held high.

Robbie passed him, shaking his head. "You have this all wrong, sir." Then he picked up speed, following after Julia at a lope. "Julia!"

She didn't even pause.

He caught up to her. "Miss Wren, at least let me drive you home."

She didn't look at him. "I think I need to walk right now."

"May I walk with you?"

She gave an exasperated huff. "Is there any way to stop you?"

"Not generally." He fell into step beside her. "Don't let old Bushy upset you. I think he's just hoping for an easy answer. He doesn't generally have to put up with any actual crime in Tuxedo Park so the prospect must be daunting."

She stopped and turned to face him. "Do you believe him?"

Robbie solemnly turned to face her and reached for her hand. "Not even for a moment." She'd been clipping along so fast, they were already out of sight of the clubhouse. He wanted to draw her into his arms again. Stroke her hair. Reassure himself again that she was fine and whole. He settled for taking her hand in his and raising it to his lips.

She turned forward quickly and pulled her hand free, resuming her march. But not so quickly that he missed the glimmer of tears on her cheeks. Tears? She was crying. He'd never seen her cry. He wasn't sure what to do. But he knew she had her pride. He elected not to notice. "Did, uh, did anyone know you were going to be at the shed?"

It was a moment before she replied. "Most everyone who was at practice this evening, I would guess." She rubbed her temple. "It wasn't a secret."

"Did anyone pay special attention to your plans?"

"I—I don't think so."

Robbie inhaled. "And you didn't see anyone or hear anything?"

"No. I already said. I never had a suspicion in the world that anyone was around the shed. But I'll tell you, they must have lit that fire the moment I was out of sight for it to have gone up like it did."

Robbie sighed. "I think it's time we cancel the whole thing. Forget about the play. It's not worth someone getting hurt over."

She shook her head. "No. No you can't do that."

"I can. It's getting too dangerous."

She threw her hands in the air. "We don't even know this is about the play."

He cocked an eyebrow at her. "First a script is burned, and then the props, and you're not sure what it's about?"

"Well." She sighed. "That does look suspicious, but we shouldn't jump to conclusions. Like whether it was a Townie or a Parkie." She waggled her eyebrows significantly.

"And what if the next thing they set fire to is your house?"

"*A.* That doesn't have anything to do with the play, so it's unlikely, and *B.,* that possibility is more reason why we should not turn a blind eye to this. Who knows who is behind this and what is driving them? If we do nothing, then who is to say what will happen the next time they feel offended or thwarted or whatever is going on in their twisted brain."

"But now the police are on it. They can take care of catching whoever is behind this. That is their job."

"And Bush is looking at me as some delusional female who is making a bid for attention." She tilted her head back and gazed up at the stars that were winking into being. Her black eye had faded to a sickly green and she looked exhausted. "Please, Robbie, if we don't do something, then everyone is going to chalk the arson up to the most convenient person. That's me. I'm a Townie and I'm handy. I can't live with a cloud like that over me. What if word was to get back to Barnard? I could be expelled."

Robbie groaned, his resolve wavering.

She laid a hand on his arm. "Please, Robbie."

"Okay." He held his hands up in surrender. "Okay, but we have to be extremely careful. We don't know what this person is capable of. Or rather we do. And it's scary."

"Oh, thank you." She surprised him by grabbing him in a brief hug. She pulled away quickly. "Sorry, sometimes I get carried away." She cleared her throat. "What do you think we should do?"

Caught up in trying to think of a way to get her to hug him again, he was slow to respond. "I suppose we have a play to put on. That means we will need new props and scenery."

"Are you still convinced it was a Townie?"

"Are you still convinced it was a Parkie?"

Julia sighed. "I don't know who it is. I don't want it to be a Townie, but at this point I don't think we can afford to rule anyone out."

"Or anyone in. We have to consider everyone as a potential suspect."

"Ooh, a 'suspect.' That sounds very official."

"I'm an official sort of person."

"Since when?"

"Since I started taking this seriously." They were coming into the village now, past the train station and post office. "I went into the city today."

She stilled. "Oh?"

"I learned through some friends there that Friedrich has attended some anarchist meetings." The pain on her face made him want to do just about anything to erase it. He hurried on. "Not one of the violent groups, and he only visited a handful of times, at least that the police know about. He hasn't been to a meeting in nearly a year."

She lowered her head, and the brim of her boater hid her expression from him. "So it really could be Friedrich." It wasn't a question, and it didn't seem meant for him, so Robbie stayed quiet, allowing her to absorb the blow in peace.

At last she lifted her head. "If it's Friedrich we still need to know."

"I've had an idea."

"Yes?"

"On Saturday I'll have everyone from the theatrical association over for a prop picnic."

"A prop picnic?"

"Yes. We'll act as if we're making a lark of it. We'll get together and paint new scenery and gather new props. They'll love it, because it will be something different. And we'll love it because it will give us an opportunity to ask questions. Everyone is going to be talking about the fire anyway, and it'll give us an opportunity to hear what they have to say."

"All right. Let's do it."

They had reached her house by then and Robbie tipped his hat as she drew away. "Thank you again, Robbie." Her sweet words were like a lightning strike slipping through his defenses and finding a place to pierce him through.

His throat tightened and he nodded. "Be careful."

"You, too."

She hurried up the walk and went inside, leaving him with his hand resting on the white picket fence and his heart floating up somewhere about his ears. And that was his problem. He was thinking with his heart instead of his head. She was right that they needed to figure out who was behind all this. But he'd be hanged if he was going to let Julia get hurt because of it. There had to be some way to draw the fire to himself.

Chapter 13

Julia was making a strawberry soda the next afternoon when she overheard a policeman telling his sweetheart that Chief Bush had officially declared the fire an accident. It was believed that the fumes of the paint cans and turpentine had somehow spontaneously combusted due to the heat. Never mind that the heat of the day had long since passed. Unofficially the story going around was that Julia must have knocked something over, or unwittingly loosened a cap of some kind when she was putting props away. And that this led to the fire and explosion.

The theory made no sense and Julia raved to Minna about it when she caught her at the post office mailing a package for Mrs. Vines.

"I agree that it makes no sense, but what are we to do?" Minna asked plaintively. "They are powerful and we are not. They will blame whoever they like to get out of embarrassment."

Julia leaned her head closer. "Minna, I need to know the name of the girl with the crazy mistress. Please. I won't get her into trouble. I just want to talk to her."

Minna sighed. "Can't you just cancel the play? Make all this go away?"

"I'm not going to let it go at that, Minna. I refuse to live the rest of my life hounded by rumors that I'm an unstable arsonist."

Minna cocked her head. "It will be difficult to find a husband."

Undoubtedly true, but not the point Julia had been trying to make. Still she nodded her head and tried to look woebegone.

"All right." Minna sighed and threw up her hands. "It is Annie Menuto."

"Annie? That poor little mouse? I bet she's terrified."

"Exactly." Minna grabbed her hand. "Don't make it worse for her."

"I promise." Julia made an X across her chest. "Wait. Doesn't she work for the Scotts?"

"Yes."

That meant that Geraldine was the young woman who had ravaged her own dress with scissors. A little thrill surged through her, though Julia couldn't say she was particularly surprised. She caught Minna's eye and at her glower raised her hands in a gesture of innocence.

"Your mind is working, I can see it."

"You would prefer I didn't think through the problem? I already promised I will be very very careful. I'm just going to talk to her. Nothing more."

Minna's glare was acid. But then her face relaxed. "In that case this is her afternoon off. You could probably entice her into the ice cream shop with the promise of a sundae. But you better make it a big one."

Julia threw her arms around Minna and kissed her cheek.

Laughing, her friend continued. "With lots of whipped cream and an extra cherry."

Grinning, Julia whirled and hurried back to the ice cream parlor. Minna was right, Annie would pass right by the shop on her way home. It was the perfect opportunity to collar her.

Lying in wait, but trying to be inconspicuous about it, Julia once more took to polishing the plate glass.

"What is your obsession with them windows lately?"

Her father's words immediately behind her made her jump. "I just think that the shop looks more inviting if the windows aren't smudgy."

"Mmm hmm." Patently unconvinced, he wiped down one of the wrought iron and marble tables. "All this gazing out the window wouldn't have something to do with Robert Malcolm would it?"

"Robbie?" She spun around at that. "No, not at all."

Thank goodness the only customers at the moment were bent over a shared malted and paying her not a whit of attention. Her cheeks burned anyway.

Pop remained bent over the table, scrubbing furiously at some bit of stickiness. "Seems like since that fellow roped you into this play I've hardly seen you, and when I do, you're floating around with your head in the clouds." Finally he looked up. "I just don't want you to get hurt. They're not like us."

"Oh, Pop, that's where you're wrong." Julia hopped down from the step stool and slid into the table's iron seat then reached for his hand. "They're no better than us, and they're no worse. They're people. Folks thinking that we're all different is what causes most of the problems around this place."

He covered her hand with his. "I worry about you, Julie Bean. It's a father's prerogative."

"I know, Pop. But I wasn't hurt and the police said that the fire was an accident. There's no reason to go blaming the incident on Robbie Malcolm, or assigning me a broken heart quite yet." Even if he did make her heart beat too fast.

"Be careful, that's all I ask."

"I promise I will." Julia leaned over and kissed his cheek.

From the corner of her eye she caught sight of a figure moving out in the street. She whirled. It was Annie. "Sorry, Pop. I've got to run. I'll be right back."

She heard his sigh as she hurried away, but didn't look back.

Out in the street she hailed Annie.

The girl looked around as if wondering who could be calling her.

Julia called again and she turned. "I know this is your afternoon off, but do you have a few minutes, Annie? I'd like to talk to you over a sundae if you can spare the time."

"I've already told Mrs. Hollis that I can't join the church choir, I can't get away for the practices." Annie's cheeks turned extra pink and her fingers knotted themselves together.

"It's nothing to do with the choir."

"Oh, all right then." Agreeably, Annie walked with Julia back to the ice cream parlor.

Julia went straight behind the counter and made the

most enticing sundae she could, then joined Annie at one of the tables.

Annie dug right in. "Mmm. I always said your parlor had the best ice cream in the world."

"I'm glad you like it." Julia clasped her hands in front of her. "Have you heard about the fire and all the strange things that have been going on around here?"

"Oh yes, it's all over the village, and the Park, too. People are saying the strangest things." Annie looked up with wide eyes. "I didn't believe a word of it."

"Thank you." Julia's eyes brimmed with unexpected tears and she blinked them away. "That's what I wanted to talk to you about though. I feel like I need to do something about it. And the only thing I can think is to try to figure out who really set the fires."

"I thought Chief Bush said it was an accident."

"He did, but after the fire on my porch, I have to keep looking. Otherwise people are going to think I'm some sort of lunatic."

Annie's eyes were wide and she gulped another huge mouthful of ice cream. "How are you gonna figure out something the police didn't?"

Julia grinned. "By making a lot of sundaes and asking a lot of questions."

Annie blinked. "You mean you want to ask me questions?"

Julia nodded and made sure her voice wouldn't carry. "Specifically about Geraldine."

Annie's head shook side to side in slow cadence as if she couldn't quite believe the foolhardiness of what she'd just heard. "You oughtn't get on the wrong side of Miss Geraldine."

"I know. And I don't wish to do anything that would

get you in trouble with your employer. I just wanted to ask you about your impressions of her. I promise not to go telling tales. But I understand that she can be…difficult."

"That's a word for it I suppose. But it's as much as my job's worth to talk about Miss Geraldine."

Julia swallowed back her impatience. "I understand." She edged her thumbnail across the pattern in the marble, keeping her eyes downcast. "I'm—it's that I'm afraid someone will get hurt. All these fires."

Annie glanced around the room, looking trapped and as if she regretted the sundae now. "Do you think Miss Geraldine could hurt somebody?"

"I don't know." Julia leaned across the table, to catch the girl's eye. "I won't know unless someone is willing to speak the truth. If she's not guilty, then you'd be doing her a favor by eliminating her from suspicion."

Annie snorted. "I don't think a word I've got to say about her is going to do that."

Julia pounced. "Then she is violent?"

Annie bit her lip briefly then nodded. "And mean-spirited."

"In what way?"

"What do you mean?"

"Well, is it at certain times or occasions? What brings it out?"

"Not getting her own way is what brings it out. Her poor parents live in mortal dread of her tantrums. If she were my daughter I'd never tolerate it, but they cater to her every whim." Annie's lip curled in disgust, an expression Julia had never seen on her face before.

"And what happens if she doesn't get what she wants?"

Now that the floodgates were open, Annie seemed

downright eager to talk. "You'd cry to see the way she carries on. Throwing things or dashing them to the ground, to destroy them. Beautiful, expensive things, too. She ordered a gown from New York and when it came it wasn't the right shade of blue. She took scissors to it and shredded it."

"Have you seen her in one of these rages?"

"Many a time. And I can tell you she don't like you one bit. The other evening she came home and she was actually swearing. I've never seen the like. The word lady gets applied very loosely these days."

"Do you know where she was last night? After the play practice?"

"The family was invited to a dinner party with the Julliards, I believe. She come home from the practice early and I helped her get ready."

Julia raised an eyebrow. "Do you often assist her?"

Annie nodded. "It's good training and one day I mean to be a lady's maid. It'd be a big step up from parlor maid."

"Did she smell of turpentine last night?"

"Turpentine? No, not that I noticed."

Julia bit back her disappointment. She'd been so sure. Then again that wasn't necessarily conclusive. "What about smoke?"

Annie shook her head.

None of this quite made sense. Geraldine sounded just like the sort of person who might decide to commit arson if it would help her get what she wanted. But how could she have started the fire if she was at a dinner party?

Hands tucked in his pockets, and whistle on his lips, Robbie surveyed the lawn. Footmen in bottle-green livery and maids in crisp black-and-white scuttled about putting the finishing touches on the buffet tables, or plumping pillows to be strewn artistically on the picnic blankets. Beyond them, swaddled in the emerald of the valley, Tuxedo Lake glimmered placidly. He longed for his camera, but managed to suppress the desire. He had to focus.

The day was perfect and with any luck he would be able to identify the culprit behind all these incidents. Somebody must have seen or heard something. They probably didn't know it had any significance. Luckily, with the right bait, everyone liked to talk.

"Robert."

He turned. "Yes, Mother?"

No one ever seemed to stand as straight as she did. "Is that what you're wearing?"

He looked down at his gray flannel suit. "Either I'm wearing it, or it's wearing me."

"Do be serious, Robert, you can't host an event in that old thing."

"I've told you a dozen times that this is not a formal gathering. We're supposed to be painting scenery and creating props and whatnot. I told everyone to wear sloppy old togs."

She closed her eyes, a look of deep weariness etched on her face. "What will the neighbors think, Robbie?"

"They'll thank me for not letting their daughters smear paint on their newest and most expensive Worth day dresses."

"Don't be so certain of that. Young ladies want to be seen at advantage, not covered in paint and gallivanting about in clothes that should have been given to the servants two seasons ago."

"Ah, but if they can catch the eye of an eligible young man in…gasp…outmoded togs, then they must be something special indeed. It will be a point of pride."

She shook her head and looked past him to the lake, but a hint of a smile flirted with the corner of her mouth. He leaned over and kissed her cheek. "I promise not to disgrace the Malcolm name."

"Well that's something, I suppose. And more than I expected."

He laughed.

A respectful throat cleared and he turned to find Mr. Hollister, the butler. "Miss Wren, sir."

He stepped to one side, and Julia was revealed. She looked fresh as a spring morning in a crisp pale blue shirtwaist and skirt, with her hair piled up and bound by a wide black velvet ribbon. Not to mention much more practical than his mother in her layers and layers of diaphanous white lace.

"Julia." Robbie smiled, and extended a hand to her. Beside him, he felt his mother stiffen at his use of Julia's given name.

He took Julia's hand and deftly maneuvered her in front of his mother. "Mother, may I present Miss Julia Wren."

Julia made a slight curtsy. "It's a pleasure to meet you, Mrs. Malcolm. Although I'm afraid I may have arrived too early."

Robbie brushed away her concern. "Not at all. You are right on time. Anyone coming after you I shall consider late."

"Miss Wren, your name is familiar, but I am having trouble placing you." His mother's smile was fixed. "I don't believe I know your family."

"No?" Julia smiled, "And here I thought everyone for miles around came into the ice cream shop. I suppose this is a lesson to me in hubris."

"Wren's Ice Cream? Then Mr. Wren is your father?"

"Oh, then you have been in? I'm delighted that my pride shall remain unscathed."

His mother looked less than enchanted and before she could say something offensive, Robbie broke in. "Miss Wren has graciously allowed us to use her play for our production."

"Her play? I thought it was *The Tempest*."

"Oh no," Robbie waggled his eyebrows at her. "It's based loosely on *The Tempest* but is a modern telling. I think the Park *grandees* will be given a lot to ponder when they see it."

"Robbie—" The persistent note of worry that filled his mother's tone when she spoke to him was back. Luckily half a dozen Parkies emerged onto the veranda and he was able to excuse himself in order to greet his guests.

"Miss Wren, perhaps you will join me. I know everyone is keen to get your vision for the way the sets should be designed."

She nodded graciously and he offered his arm. In a low voice she said, "I know you will disagree, but if you can, try to find out whether Geraldine was really at the Julliard's dinner party. And if she was, did she leave for any significant amount of time."

He looked down at her in surprise, brows drawn together, but he couldn't ask any questions. They had already reached the other guests.

A few of the girls had dressed practically, like Julia. Most of them had followed his mother's example and wore floaty gowns that were certain to be ruined before the day was through. Or else would render the wearer incapable of offering any sort of help with anything. Ah well, they wouldn't have been of much use anyway.

Soon everyone had arrived and Robbie had doled out assignments. He made sure to keep a good ratio of fellows to girls, and to group those of similar tastes and inclinations together. It was as bad as determining a seating plan for a fifty-person dinner party. Maybe worse.

But everything went along swimmingly once he had people situated. Some were painting scenery on the stretched lengths of linen. Others reclined on the picnic blankets and fussed with smaller props. At their leisure they strolled about the long banquet tables and helped themselves to the tea sandwiches, cold salmon, and galantine of veal, fruit consommés and delicate cakes and tarts that beckoned tantalizingly. Footmen and maids circulated among the guests removing unwanted dishes, refilling glasses or fetching glue and beads.

There was a great deal of chattering and as Robbie worked his way through the various groups, keeping them on task and providing encouragement or inspiration as necessary, he kept his ears open for any discussion of the fire.

He didn't even have to try to scramble to find a way to introduce the topic into conversation. Most everyone wanted to speculate about it. It was a piece of cake to ask where people had been when the fire occurred.

He could see Julia moving among the different groups, and knew she was asking questions and probing for information as well. What had she meant by asking after Geraldine? Is that who she suspected of being the arsonist? It sounded absurd. Arson wasn't really a woman's kind of act, was it?

Although now that he thought about it, there was no reason it couldn't be. It didn't require a great deal of strength, or a particular mechanical knowledge that a young woman might not have gained. It mostly required access to matches and a certain disregard for others' property and safety. If the arson was related to the play, as they thought, then it also signaled an unhealthy mind. Obsessive and mean-spirited. These traits weren't confined to men, either.

Robbie looked about at the prettily dressed, well-mannered young ladies all around him with a new consideration.

Chapter 14

Julia fought down her sense of alienness and submerged herself in the personality she had elected to assume for the day. Insouciant, witty, an excellent listener and slightly nosy. It was a sort of mask that kept her from revealing too much of her real self. Almost as good as wearing armor.

While Geraldine was flirting with Hugh Dellafield over a swath of canvas that was being painted to resemble a stormy sea, Julia took the opportunity to claim a seat by Harriet on one of the picnic blankets.

"Hullo, Harriet. That's quite an interesting goblet you're making."

Harriet looked from the gold trim she was pasting to the cup, her eyes narrowed in suspicion. "What's wrong with it?"

"Nothing." Julia straightened her skirts around her feet. "I think it looks sort of Mesopotamian."

Still eyeing her as if she expected an insult to come winging her way, Harriet continued gluing on the bit of trim. A silence began to bloom in the space between them. Harriet's taciturnity was elbows out, staving off conversation as effectively as if she had actually proclaimed a disinclination to talk.

As she searched through bits of ribbon, rhinestones and beads, Julia cast about for a way to introduce the topic of the fire. Something she hadn't had to do up until now.

Just as the silence reached ungainly proportions Robbie dropped down beside her on the blanket. "This party has turned out to be a great deal more work than I ever would have believed. Everyone seems to need to be told what to do." He reached up and tweaked Harriet's nose. "Except for you, my dear. Here you are working diligently on—" he peered at the goblet in her hand "—drinking vessels of all kinds."

A pink flush tinged her cheek and she ducked her chin ever so slightly. "I thought it might work well for old Prosper to have a goblet."

"Perfect. Prosper definitely requires a goblet. It's the finishing touch that we needed. I can't wait to start waving it around majestically."

Harriet's giggle was high and fluting. "You can't wave it around, it's Prosper's."

"I can't?" Robbie looked horrified. "Then I insist that you make one for me as well. Come along." He clapped his hands in her direction. "Hop to it. I want one just as goblety."

Julia stayed quiet, watching Robbie's deft handling of Harriet. He knew these people as she never would. There was no question about it. It didn't take him long to charm Harriet out of her shell. And when he did, she looked quite pretty in her white flounces.

Robbie's presence drew others and soon they had half a dozen men and women sitting daringly together on the blankets and desultorily decorating all sorts of odds and ends, from cups, to a scepter, to a little three-legged stool.

One of the others brought up the fire, and the subject took hold of the conversation as quickly as the fire had gripped the shed. Despite the official explanation that it had been an accident, it was still too exciting and mysterious to be relinquished as a source of conversation.

Everyone seemed to have a theory. But most of them had been nowhere near the clubhouse or the shed when the fire broke out.

"And where were you, Miss Harriet?" Robbie handed her a tiny nosegay of wired violets to add to the fine old cut glass decanter she was obscuring in miscellaneous bric-a-brac.

"My family dined with the Ellisons at the clubhouse that evening. It was quite the event."

"Why, then you practically had front row seats," Robbie said.

Immediately a chorus of "Did you see anything?" started up.

Harriet seemed to puff up a little under the attention. "I did happen to see something that might have been important."

"What?" Charlie leaned forward.

From the look on Harriet's face, she hadn't been the center of this much attention in a very long time. Her cheeks were flushed and her eyes sparkled. "It might not have been anything at all."

"Of course it was something if you've remembered it," Robbie said.

Geraldine had wandered over to stand just behind Robbie. She listened in with a sour expression on her face.

"It was a fellow. A Townie. One of the Beyerses' servants. Chauffeur I think from his uniform. His name is Friedrich." She seemed to think she was losing her audience. She rushed on. "He was running away from the direction of the shed. A minute later I heard the shout about the fire and headed over there. But by that time the whole thing was engulfed in flames. It was awful."

"It was dark out, Harriet, how could you possibly have recognized some servant? Especially without your glasses." Geraldine's tone was waspish.

Harriet's pretty flush turned a shade darker. "My eyesight was good enough to see you hurrying across the lawns that evening, too."

Geraldine gave a sharp inhale. "You're ridiculous. I was dining with the Julliard's that evening. I know you're vain, but you really shouldn't leave the house without those glasses." She swept away, her skirts smacking against Julia's back as she pivoted on her heel.

Julia met Robbie's gaze and a flash of understanding passed between them. Was Geraldine hiding something? With raised eyebrows and one or two snickers the others drifted away in her wake, leaving Julia and Robbie alone with Harriet once more.

Harriet's jaw was pugnacious as she plucked a strand of beads from the pile without even looking at it. "Please don't feel I'm keeping you."

Julia didn't make any move to leave. "Are you all right? Have you and Geraldine had a falling-out?"

Harriet sniffed. "She can't stand to see anyone else in the limelight. She'll be fine once she is the center of attention again."

"But what of you?"

"I'm used to her." Harriet dropped the string of beads back into the pile. "Robbie, why is the play still going on?"

At the abrupt change in subject, Robbie glanced up from the bell he was adorning. "Pardon?"

"With everything that's happened, why are we still putting on her play?" She gestured with her chin at Julia.

"Why wouldn't we?"

Harriet tilted her head. "I heard that the fire at her house was caused by a script being set on fire, and now the prop shed was set aflame. And let's not forget about your car accident. It seems like this play is cursed. And I for one would think that you'd be concerned." Cheeks flushed and eyes snapping, she stood and stalked away to one of the banquet tables while Julia gaped after her.

"I wonder who she heard that from?" said Robbie.

"If I were inclined to guess, I'd say Geraldine Scott." Julia faced him, willing him to acknowledge that she had been right to be suspicious of Geraldine.

"And what of her comment about Friedrich running from the fire?"

There was that. Her shoulders slumped a little. "I think we have to look into them both."

He stuck out his hand and they shook on it. They were agreed. She just wished her fingers didn't tingle so much when they touched his.

* * *

Robbie spent much of the next morning lolling about the Park grounds. Having been unable to come up with a single useful thing to do, he headed for the ice cream parlor. He'd been going there so frequently he was starting to feel like a homing pigeon. Though if truth be told, the beacon he was homing in on wasn't the parlor, it was Julia. She was like true north, magnetically tugging at him, no matter where she was.

Feeling contemplative he left his car in the garage and set out on foot, swinging his cane jauntily and whistling as he walked. The exercise would no doubt do him good. There had been the tiniest nip in the air that morning. Fall was just around the corner and with it, Julia would be leaving again. Going off to Barnard and all her adventures in the great metropolis. Caught up in her studies and her friends, her life would take on a new rhythm. A rhythm that didn't include him. The idea was uncomfortable and slightly frustrating, like having something caught in his teeth.

He could go stay in his family's New York City home, too, but proximity wouldn't necessarily cause her to make space for him in her life. She didn't need him. She was independent and strong. Had already created a life for herself there without reference to anyone or anything but her own desires. How could he shoehorn his way in? He wasn't sure about anything but his own determination to find a way.

His reverie was interrupted by an explosion. He jumped at least a foot. Looking over his shoulder he realized the Beyerses' car had backfired. Friedrich was behind the wheel. The fellow didn't so much as nod at Robbie as he passed. In his wake the vehicle kicked up

dust and grit that set Robbie to coughing. He blinked.
Had there even been any passengers? The car was already so far away he couldn't tell.

Good mood trampled, he grumbled the rest of the
way to the ice cream parlor, only to find the same car
parked outside.

Choking down an oath he stomped up to the porch
and just managed to restrain himself from slamming
the door. Inside, at the end of the long counter, Friedrich stood staring stonily ahead, while Julia talked to
him in an undertone, her gestures tight and pointed.

Instinct warred with cunning, and Robbie elected
to approach softly in order to hear what was going on.

"—been avoiding me, Friedrich. I can't believe you'd
even bother to deny it."

"I do not wish to argue with you, Julia. Can you just
get the ice cream for Mrs. Beyers? She is worried about
her luncheon and wished me to hurry."

"I don't care about Mrs. Beyers's domestic tribula-
tions." Julia jabbed a finger at his chest. "There have
been too many 'accidents,' Friedrich. And you *have*
been avoiding me."

"I for one can't imagine why anyone would wish to
avoid Miss Wren." Robbie stepped up smoothly beside
the chauffeur.

A sneer started on Friedrich's face, but he managed
to smooth it quickly away. "As you say, sir."

Robbie smiled lazily. "We're very interested, Friedrich. What were you doing by the prop shed the night
of the fire?"

"Me? Near the shed?"

"Don't bother trying to deny it. You were seen."

Friedrich didn't even look at Robbie, he was focused

on Julia. She looked as if she were being tortured by the disbelief in Friedrich's eyes. Her face was drawn, her eyes red-rimmed and positively boring a hole in Friedrich.

The silence stretched between them, taut. "I don't answer to you," Friedrich said, his voice harsh.

"I thought I knew you. I thought you were my friend." Julia's eyes brimmed with tears.

"You don't wish my friendship. You wish him. You want to be a Parkie." His voice dripped with disdain.

Robbie's heart leapt a little at the words. Could it be true? Could she love him?

Friedrich stepped forward, looming over Julia. Jaw clenched, Robbie quietly stepped to her side. Friedrich didn't so much as glance at him. "Why don't you just leave them alone? You should stop consorting with them or you might get hurt."

Julia was white and haggard as if she were an invalid. She raised her chin though. "It's true, isn't it? You're an anarchist."

"What do you have planned for those of us who don't share your views?" Robbie demanded. "Will you be planting bombs soon like the anarchists in Europe?"

From behind Julia, a stout worker in a striped dress and apron emerged from the back with two large cartons of ice cream. "Here we are."

Friedrich moved to snatch them from the girl. "You will kindly send the bill to Mrs. Beyers as usual." Then he stalked away, letting the door smack closed behind him.

Julia drew a shaky breath and put a hand to her middle.

"Are you all right?" Robbie hated seeing the toll the confrontation had taken on her.

"I didn't want to believe it possible." She gave a hollow little laugh. "But it appears that you were right about him."

Robbie reached for her hand. "We don't know that. It's obvious he has his pride. Maybe he just got his back up over the allegations." Was he actually defending the great grouch, now? But he would have done anything to erase the stricken look from her face.

"I don't know anymore. Maybe he does think I've betrayed my class. My kind." Her words were quiet and a bit fractured. But then she straightened. "So what can I do for you?"

"I—" Robbie didn't really have a good answer for her. "Nothing. I wanted to see you is all."

She looked at him then. Really looked. Their gazes clashed together like cymbals. Her cheeks turned pink, the color banishing her paleness. He tried to read the expression in her face. To gauge her reaction. Abruptly she cast her eyes down, breaking the electric current that seemed to buzz between them. "As long as you're here perhaps you'd like a malted?"

He wanted a whole lot more. "Sounds good."

Silence stretched out between them, unwieldy as an octopus in a net bag. Julia soon slid a tall glass across to him, then seemed to take refuge in serving several other customers. Robbie sipped his malted slowly. He watched her interacting with her patrons. Smiling and gracious. The desire to photograph her welled up in him. He wanted to capture her in all her moods. To see if film would be able to house the intensity of her gaze or the sweetness of her smile. She stayed away for a long time. Full of longing, he waited until she ran out of distractions. Eventually she drifted within speaking distance again.

"You want to talk about it?" Robbie asked in a low voice.

"No. Yes." She sighed. "I do, but not now. I need to think it through first."

He pushed away from his stool. "All right. Let me know when you want to talk. Anytime."

She nodded without raising her eyes to meet his. He had taken three steps when she spoke. "Thank you."

He turned back to her.

"Thank you for not pressing. I'll talk about it when I'm ready, but until then—"

He nodded. "Until then." And it wasn't a question. It was a promise.

Before he knew it he was climbing the broad steps to his veranda. The walk home had passed in a blur, his mind completely occupied as he'd strolled. Although it was all a jumbled mess. The fires, Julia, the play. What he was going to do with the rest of his life. He couldn't seem to tease any single strand from the tangle.

He let himself into the house and headed out to the back porch, when a gruff voice stopped him.

"That's the whole point, Caroline."

Robbie stopped in his tracks. Father was in Tuxedo Park. And it wasn't a weekend. This boded no good. Even as he considered how best to make a dash for it, his father emerged from the morning room.

"Ah, there you are. Kind of you to interrupt your day of lollygagging in order to see your family."

"Good afternoon, Father."

"Where have you been?"

"I took a stroll."

"You didn't take that wretched camera with you." It was no question. It was an ultimatum.

Robbie clenched his hands into fists at his side. "I did not."

"Well that's something I suppose. Come in here." His father turned on his heel and moved back into the morning room.

Reluctantly, Robbie followed. "Good afternoon, Mother."

She raised her cool cheek for a kiss and he bent over her dutifully. "I'm sure a walk did you good. No one seems to walk anymore. Everyone wants to flit about in those dreadful, noisy, smelly autos."

Unwilling to spend more time than absolutely necessary being criticized on a gorgeous summer afternoon, Robbie turned to his father. "Did you need something?"

"Your mother has been telling me about a girl. An unsuitable girl."

Robbie was suddenly glad that he hadn't chosen to sit down. "Oh?"

"I'm not paying off another angry father."

"You didn't have to pay off the first one. I never had a thing to do with the girl except a moonlight stroll."

"That is not what people were saying."

"People used to say the earth was flat. Saying it didn't make it so." The blood was rushing in his ears, a loud thrumming that threatened to drown out all other sounds. "If you had believed me instead of them, we could have proved them false somehow."

"There would always have been those who chose to believe the stories."

"Like you."

His father banged a fist on the table. "It was best to hush it up and make them go away. I don't wish to re-hash that sordid affair. I wish to speak to you about this Wren girl."

Robbie clasped his hands behind his back, afraid of what he might do if his father were to insult Julia. "Tread carefully, Father."

"I! I tread carefully?" His father was on his feet now. Rage had his face maroon, and his old-fashioned mutton chop whiskers bristling. "How dare you speak to me in such a manner."

Mother's voice shrilled above his father's basso. "Garrick. Garrick, remember your heart." She fluttered a handkerchief at them. "My nerves cannot bear another scene."

Father grudgingly lowered himself back down in his seat.

And at another imperious wave of his mother's hand, Robbie sat, too.

"You see," muttered his father, "your antics with this girl are straining your mother's nerves."

"What antics?" Robbie demanded. "I cannot think of a thing I've done all summer that can properly be called an antic."

"You know very well that we cannot approve of this girl you've taken up company with."

"And why is that?"

"Whatever else you may be, you are not stupid. She's a Townie."

"Her father is a business owner, just as mine is. He is a respected member of their community, just as mine is. He is a local employer, just as mine is. It is true his success is on a smaller scale. But what about her is so very unsuitable?"

"We both know she is only interested in your money."

"Completely unlike any of the Park girls." Robbie snorted his derision. "You know nothing of her. At least meet her before you consign her to the status of scheming light-skirts."

"Watch your tongue. Your mother is present."

"So it's all right for you to imply such things about an innocent young woman. But not all right for me to point out that that's what you're doing."

"No. You are being deliberately obtuse. This is as bad as your obsession with those ridiculous cameras." His father pulled at his whiskers. "I suppose I must handle it the same way then. So be it. Give her up and choose someone suitable this season, or you're cut off. You'll never get a dime. Then we'll see whether she sticks around."

Robbie was so angry that his vision seemed to narrow to a tiny pinprick. It was only by God's grace that he didn't strike his father. Instead he managed a curt bow of his head. "Thank you, Father. If you're quite done, I have a few obligations I must take care of this afternoon." Without waiting for a reply he spun on his heel and left.

Nearly choking on his fury he marched out into the gardens and beyond, striding deeper and deeper into the woods. It had come down to this. He could no longer choose only what was pleasant or convenient.

Julia sat with her elbow on her knee and her chin propped in her hand as the scene took shape. There was something enchanting about it. Maybe she should become a real playwright. Seeing a story come to life was amazing. The Parkies weren't half bad actors either.

Tommy Beyers crossed in front of her and sat a few seats away, paging through his script. Julia's focus on the play faltered as she watched him from the corner of her eye. He was Friedrich's employer. Surely he wouldn't employ a man he didn't trust. For heaven's sake, Friedrich drove around the man's aged mother and younger sister.

On the stage Geraldine broke role, stamped her foot. "I said the line perfectly well, Robbie. It's a rotten line."

Concentration on the play thoroughly disrupted, Julia sighed and left Robbie to deal with her. Anything she had to say to Geraldine would only cause trouble. It was time to ask a few more questions. She slid over to sit next to Tommy.

"Hello, Mr. Beyers."

"Miss Wren." He set his script aside. A relieved sort of expression on his face indicated that he was more than happy to have a distraction. "I hope you aren't paying too much attention to Geraldine's ranting."

"I don't think she's really stopped since we began. I've learned to not notice." Julia straightened her skirts, settling comfortably into the seat.

"A wise strategy. If you can't beat them, ignore them." He crossed his legs, turning toward her slightly.

"It may not have been what Hannibal or Caesar would have done, but I find it effective."

He grinned. "There are worse approaches, believe me."

"You speak as if you have experience."

He cast a look at the stage that seemed equal parts longing and exasperation. "She doesn't mean it. Not really. When you get down to it, she's a sweet girl underneath."

Julia decided to reserve judgment on that score. "I think you know a friend of mine." Not the most graceful of segues.

"Oh?" He raised an eyebrow as if mildly surprised that such a thing might be possible.

"Friedrich Bauer. I believe he's your chauffeur."

"Ah yes. Good old Friedrich. You know him, you say?"

"We've known one another for years."

"I see. He's a swell chap. Quite a good driver of course."

"Yes."

The conversation seemed to flag. It was obvious that Tommy didn't know much about Friedrich. But then Tommy seemed to have a moment of inspiration. "I was just talking about him to Robbie Malcolm a few days ago. I'm afraid I'm going to have to give ol' Friedrich a raise or Malcolm will poach him."

"You have to watch out for that Malcolm."

"So I'm told. So I'm told."

Once again the conversation seemed in danger of flagging, a capital crime among this set. Tommy floundered to rescue it. "I understand you tried to save the prop shed the other night." Good. He'd gone to the most popular recent choice of topic, as she'd hoped.

"I dashed a bucket of water at it if that's what you mean." She smiled. "Were you at the club that evening?"

"No. The one night this place proves to be exciting and I was away in boring old Manhattan." He shook his head. "It's a pity."

"Oh, you must be one of those young bucks like

Robbie Malcolm who likes to drive yourself about then."

Tommy's brow furrowed. "Why do you say that?"

Julia frowned. "I understood that Friedrich was here."

"Oh no. Friedrich was with me. I always have him drive if there is a chance that I might overindulge."

"I see." Julia sat back in her chair as he prattled on about the dull evening he'd had. A moment later a halloo from stage indicated that Tommy had missed his cue and he toddled off.

Julia stayed where she was, mind aswim with possibilities. If Friedrich had been in the city with Tommy, why had Harriet said she'd seen him? It was conceivable that she had been mistaken. The Parkies were often quite cavalier about knowing who servants were. Especially other people's servants. But she had been very definite in her statement. She had called Friedrich by name. That seemed deliberate. But if so, she chose to lie. And there was the real rub. Why would Harriet have lied? And if she had lied about Friedrich, had she also lied about Geraldine?

Julia stood abruptly. She needed to talk to Robbie.

On stage the actors marked their way through the final scene. Charlie in the role of Tom Prosper was magnanimous as he freed the disgruntled Caliban from his contract, banishing the threat of another strike by his generous treatment. Julia spotted Robbie where he was mouthing the lines for the actors as needed. Geraldine sat next to him, her thigh almost brushing his, her arm linked comfortably through his. Julia's step faltered, and she was immediately surrounded by a trio of nymphs.

"Julia, this seam is splitting, and Fannie's headpiece is positively falling apart."

"Do you think the blue ribbons or the green are more nymphlike?"

"I spilled some punch on my costume, do you think my maid will be able to get it out?"

Julia raised her hands to halt the twittering. "Girls, we can sort it all, but one at a time please." Then she allowed herself to be drawn away. There was no immediate rush to talk to Robbie.

Chapter 15

Awkward silence seemed to muscle aside the air in the car, which was odd considering that it didn't have a roof. How could it possibly be stuffy?

Julia smoothed the fabric of her skirt for what seemed the hundredth time. "I—uh, think the rehearsal went fairly well."

Robbie seemed to wake from a dream. "Huh? Oh, yeah. It was fine. Just fine. They'll do all right tomorrow night."

Julia couldn't think of a thing to say in response that wouldn't sound utterly witless.

The silence began to swell again.

Robbie turned to look at her. "How do you do it?"

She blinked. "What?"

"Everything? How do you make a budget? More important how do you live on limited means? How do you shop for groceries? How do you make sure your clothes are clean? If you're in town and you want to go somewhere without a car, how do you know when an omnibus is going to come by or whether it would be quicker to take the subway?"

Julia couldn't help the smile that split her face. "You're wondering how the other half lives?"

He slowed the car. "I'm realizing that I don't know how to do a thing for myself. I've never had to. I'm practically helpless." His expression was grim, almost savage. "I don't want to be helpless."

Julia's smile faded. This was important to Robbie. Vitally important. "I'll tell you what I can. What do you want to know first?"

The look he shot her, at once fierce and proud and grateful and appealing was above all full of relief, and she knew it would have hurt him immeasurably if she had laughed at him. "How much would I absolutely need to have to live on?"

"In New York or somewhere else?"

"New York."

"You could get by very comfortably on $1,000 a year."

He swiveled his head to look at her. "That doesn't seem right. My monthly allowance is more than that."

Now she did laugh. "Pure extravagance. A male teacher makes $900 a year."

His eyes narrowed. "You seem quite well-informed about what a *male* teacher would make."

Julia tried on what she hoped was an enigmatic smile. "I do have friends outside the Park."

She could see the gears turning as he tried to decide how to respond to this sally.

"A woman makes about a third less," she added.

"But that's only about $600." He looked appalled.

Julia nodded.

"All right, tell me. How do they do it? There must be some sort of trick or something."

She shook her head. "I'm afraid this is going to be a blow. Why don't we stop by the shop and have some ice cream while I explain."

"Good idea."

A moment later Robbie pulled in front of the ice cream parlor and helped her out of the car.

Julia rummaged in her handbag for the key.

Robbie watched intently as she pulled it out and shook his head. "I just realized that I've never used a key in my entire life. There's always staff to open a door for me, usually before I've even climbed the steps, and the butler locks up at night."

She held the key out to him flat on her palm. "Consider this your first lesson in common life."

Grinning he took the key and examined it with an almost comical look of concentration. Then he scrutinized the lock. He inserted it, tried to twist it, realized his mistake and twisted it the other way. Then he tried the handle. The door opened and he ushered her inside, his grin widening. "Well teacher, did I pass with flying colors?"

"You did indeed." She brushed past him close enough to catch that clove and mint smell. Her mouth went a little dry. "What would you like for your reward?

The look he gave her, half smile and with a raised eyebrow, made her acutely aware that he had an altogether different kind of reward in mind.

She clarified. "A malted, a milkshake?"

He smiled good-naturedly and didn't press her. "I think a victory like this demands a sundae at the very least."

Her stomach aflutter, she moved through the moon-lit ice cream parlor. "It just so happens that sundaes are lesson two."

Rather than settling on a stool he joined her behind the long counter. He stood close in the relatively narrow space. Julia looked back over her shoulder. She swallowed. His nearness was very appealing. She grabbed an apron and tied it around her waist with practiced fingers. Then handed him an apron of his own. She led the way to the freezer as he fumbled to tie his in place.

She started to heft out one of the tubs of ice cream but he reached in and removed it from her hands. "If I'm going to do it. I'm going to do it well."

"All right, I'll supervise."

Together they concocted an enormous ice cream sundae complete with the Wrens' special homemade chocolate sauce, salty Spanish peanuts to balance out the sweetness, a cloud of whipped cream and a cherry on top. Julia produced two spoons and they sat down across from one another at one of the small marble-topped tables to share.

Robbie was curious about everything. All sorts of mundane things it would never have occurred to her to question. From the cost of a pound of butter—twenty-six cents—to how one went about trying to find lodgings.

Friedrich would have been all derision, looking at Robbie's ignorance of these matters as a character flaw. Julia felt that his desire to remedy his ignorance was endearing. She had liked him since she'd gotten over her initial anger about being roped into the play scheme. And she had to admit that she had found him attractive long before that. But the delicate new growth of friendship that had sprouted between them seemed to be sending roots deep into the soil of her heart as they talked and laughed over their shared sundae in the light of a single lamp.

Julia thought she saw movement out beyond the plate glass. Her head whipped up and she peered outside, but try as she might she couldn't see a thing.

"Is something wrong?" He turned to peer out the window, too.

"No. I thought—" She shook her head. "Robbie, I forgot to tell you what I found out tonight." Briefly she outlined what Tommy had told her.

Robbie sat back, crossing his arms when she was done. "So why would Harriet lie?"

"Exactly." Julia pushed away from the table and picked up the now empty ice cream dish. "And how would she even know Friedrich's name?"

"Yes, I noted that, too. There aren't many Parkies who can name their acquaintances' servants."

"But what purpose could be served by the falsehood?"

Robbie followed her to the sink. "Either she wished to point suspicion at him specifically, or she wished to divert suspicion from somewhere else. Do you think she was trying to protect Geraldine? They've been the closest friends since they were tykes."

"Which would make sense except that she then told everyone that she saw Geraldine there, too."

"Maybe that was just because she got aggravated

with her and lashed out. Or do you think she was trying to protect someone else?"

"I don't know what to think. Is there someone else she is particularly close too?"

Robbie took hold of the handle of the water pump, working it until water gushed into the sink. A look of grim satisfaction crossed his features. As if by each simple skill he executed, he was moving toward some goal. "I can't think of anyone. No one but herself that is."

"What do you mean?"

"Well, she and Geraldine have always been absorbed in themselves and their own affairs."

"Then to your other point, do you think it was an attempt to cast suspicion on Friedrich?"

"I have to go back to why she would do it. She's petty, but I don't think she'd deliberately lie about someone unless she thought there would be some benefit to her."

"That's where I get stumped. It seems a vengeful sort of thing to do." Julia sighed and gave another swipe at the bowl. "Why would she pick on a neighbor's chauffeur whom she presumably barely knows?" She reached for a spoon but stopped midgesture. "That's not quite true. Friedrich used to work for the Vineses. He was a groom in their stables. He left about three years ago and went to work for the Beyers while his sister Minna stayed. It was rather abrupt. Although I don't think he was sacked."

"Do you think he left because of some trouble with Harriet?"

"A week ago I would have said no, but now I don't know. I feel like I don't know him at all. Or not nearly as well as I thought I did. I—" She could feel a flush rising into her cheeks, but she carried on. "I had thought that he was interested in me."

Robbie took up a dish towel and began to dry the few dishes. "Then what if he wasn't the cause of the problem? I mean, if you say he wasn't sacked. What if he chose to leave? What if it was because of Harriet?"

"Like Harriet was interested in him but he didn't return the affection?" Julia took the now dry bowl from him and put it away. "What would that have to do with the play and why would she be seeking revenge at this late date?"

Robbie shook his head. "Let's think about this. What if she thought she was in love with Friedrich, but he fled her advances because he cared for you? Now she is being forced to participate in a play by the very girl she blames for her failure with Friedrich. She wouldn't be happy about that."

"But it hardly seems enough to inspire arson. It was so long ago, and she doesn't seem as if she's pining for Friedrich." She accepted the ice cream scoop and put it away. "If anything when we all met at the lake, I thought she had eyes for you."

Robbie set down the towel and fumbled behind him at the knot he'd managed to tangle in the apron strings. "Me?" He gave a sharp intake of breath. "That's it. It explains it all. She did care for Friedrich, but now she's after me. And both of us ended up making our interest in you plain. She is jealous of you; which is why she has gone after you and your play."

"Harriet is jealous of me?" She scoffed. "It's Geraldine who might be said to have any sort of claim on you and she's the one who has been taking all the snipes at me. Harriet hasn't tried to put me down much." She put a hand on his arm and turned him around so that she could reach the knot.

He held still as she worked. "I'm not saying that Geraldine is all sunshine and daisies, but I think we need to think long and hard about Harriet. She has played second fiddle to Geraldine for most of her life because the Scotts are an older and richer family. And as they grew up, Geraldine was prettier and more charming. It must be hard to bear at times. Always being outshone. But I'll bet you her pride couldn't bear the idea of coming in a poor second to a Townie, and not just once, but twice."

"But arson? Surely that is too extreme."

"She didn't start with arson, remember. She started with lobbing a brick. Then she burned that script and got away with it. Each of her successes made her bolder. And the prop shed must have been the easiest of the lot. There was less chance of her being remarked upon at the Park than in the village."

"You really believe it is more likely to be Harriet than Friedrich?"

"I hate to abandon an appealing suspect," he shrugged, "but yes."

Having worked the knots free she stepped back, vaguely relieved and mightily sorry to put a more proper distance between them. He had a very nice back, with a narrow waist that tapered up to broad shoulders. He turned to face her again, a gleam of excitement in his eyes. There was something unutterably sweet in this sharing of ideas. As if they were partners. It was how she had imagined marriage.

Hands suddenly shaky, she asked, "How do we go about proving it? Chief Bush isn't going to take our word against one of the Park ladies. Especially since he's already said it was an accident."

Robbie twisted his lips in a grimace. "That will be tougher than theorizing."

The flutter of her hands at the small of his back had just about snapped Robbie's self-control. When he turned to face her the only thing that stopped him from drawing her into his arms was the worry gathered in her wide, petal-blue eyes. He cleared his throat. "We'll find a way."

Her responding smile was a gallant effort at light-heartedness. "The fires should stop after the play, right? Or at the least when I go back to school and we have nothing more to say to one another."

To cover the hollowness that gutted him at that idea, Robbie pulled a face. "You would quit the field of honor before your prize was won?"

She cocked an eyebrow. "My prize?"

"Me of course. You would leave me behind to face the likes of Harriet Vines and Geraldine Scott alone."

"Every damsel hates to abandon a knight in distress, but there are times when it seems the better part of valor."

"I'm wounded." Robbie flung his hand up to his brow in mocking despair.

"We can't have that. Perhaps you should abscond to the city as well. Surely your family has a home there? That way we can cede the field without ceding the prize."

"An admission! I knew you considered me the prize all along."

She flushed, but her smile remained. "You're quite

sure of yourself, aren't you?" She reached behind her back to untie her own apron.

He couldn't maintain the joke, and his throat ached with sincerity. "No. But I'm sure of you."

Her movements slowed, and her chin, which had been tucked down, came up as she met his eyes.

The air seemed to have been sucked from the room leaving the abnormal hush and stillness that comes in the moment before a storm hits. Robbie forged on, knowing only that he had to tell her how he felt. "I know it's a little mad. But I've never been more certain of anything." He reached to brush a tendril of hair from her temple. "I've fallen in love with you. You're everything I admire. Independent, strong and joyful. I want…." The words dried and congealed in his throat.

She was shaking her head in a small jerky back and forth motion. She backed away from him. "Maybe you think you're being kind. But you're not. It's not kindness to speak of what can never be."

"Why do you say—?" He stopped and as one, they sniffed the air. "Smoke!"

They raced through to the back room.

The crash of glass assaulted them as they entered. A broken bottle lay on the floor. All around it flames licked at the floor and walls. The door banged closed. Julia snatched up her skirts, darted past the fire and barreled out the door.

Robbie spied the fancy wrapped gift box he had brought for Julia weeks ago. He ripped off the cover. Inside, still nestled in their snug packaging, lay the fire grenades. He grabbed up two and hurled them at the blaze. Two more, and it seemed to have doused the flames. He dashed after Julia.

Bursting through the door he glanced left and right. Julia was tearing down the road, she was already past the train station, almost to the turn for the Park. He sprinted after her, and realized that she was chasing a figure.

They needed to raise the hue and cry. The fire station and the police had to be called. Robbie yelled until he was gasping for breath. One or two lights went on and he prayed that someone was acting. In the meantime, he put on a burst of speed trying to catch up with Julia.

She had no business chasing an arsonist. It was a good way to get herself hurt, or even killed. The August moon was just peeking over the hills. Whoever was ahead of them did seem to be heading for the Park, and that likely indicated it was a Parkie. The problem would be if they veered off the road into the woods. Without dogs or lanterns it would be all but impossible to find someone in the tangled wilds.

Especially someone who didn't want to be found. Although, with the fence around the Park, that tactic could pose just as much trouble for the arsonist as it did for them. Even as he thought it, the figure swung right, plunging into the woods.

Robbie knew by the sinking in his chest what Julia would do. "Wait for me!"

Julia didn't even turn her head. She dove at the shadow, tackling it. There was a thud as they crashed together to the ground. And then there was screaming and thrashing. Robbie came abreast of them and stared helplessly at the tangle for a moment. He didn't know where one of them ended and the other began. He drew nearer and got a kick in the shin for his troubles. Grunting he dove in. He got an arm around Julia's waist and all but hauled her away.

The other figure continued to flail. Her heels thudding against the ground, her head jerking back and forth. A terrible screeching wail tore from her throat to scratch at the night's peace.

"Stop it," Julia ordered. She was barely out of breath, but she sounded thoroughly annoyed.

Robbie moved to restrain the woman, but Julia put a hand on his arm and shook her head. To the figure, Julia raised her voice. "Pipe down, Harriet. We know it's you. And you're not going to get out of it by caterwauling."

On the ground the figure stilled. Instinctively Robbie reached out a hand.

Harriet accepted and with his help stood. "Thank goodness you're here, Robbie. This lunatic attacked me. I'm sure you saw it." She raised her hand to her hair and began patting her coiffure back into place.

"You're an arsonist." The sneer in Julia's voice was unmistakable even though it was difficult to discern her expression.

"Don't be ridiculous." Harriet plucked dead leaves from her sleeve, all hauteur as only a Parkie could manage.

"Why were you running?" Julia challenged.

"Because someone started chasing me." Harriet's condescension was boundless, and about to earn her a sock in the mouth. Robbie tried to position himself a little closer to Julia, just in case.

A car rattled up, its headlamps illuminating all three of them where they stood at the edge of the woods.

Chief Bush piled out. "What's all the racket?"

"Mr. Bush, I'm glad you're here." Harriet smoothed her hair. "This woman attacked me."

Julia shook her head. "You're something else, you know that? She set fire to the ice cream parlor. And she's the one who set fire to the prop shed and my porch, too."

"She's mad." Harriet shook her head. "The poor creature is fixated. She desperately wants there to be a villain so that she can cling to the little attention we Parkies have bestowed on her."

Julia took a step toward Harriet.

Chief Bush started forward. "Whoa, now!"

Robbie intervened, arm outstretched between them. "Ladies. Please."

Harriet simpered at him. "I'm glad you're here to see what she is."

"I can see what you both are." Robbie's smile back was frosty. "You're a lady of the Park."

Her chin tilted upward, a triumphant smirk flashing.

Robbie continued. "A selfish, scheming and violent, lady of the park. While Julia is gracious, kind and a lady in the true sense of the word."

Harriet gasped. "How dare you."

Robbie kept on. If his theory was right, the only way to get her to admit her role was to goad her into it, and he'd have only one chance.

"You can't bear it that I prefer her over you, can you?"

"You don't. You can't." Her jaw was set, the planes of her face hard.

"I do. She is more refined and cultured." He hit her where it would really hurt. "Prettier, and more fashionable, too."

Harriet's nostrils flared, color burning in bright splotches on her face.

Julia understood what he was up to. "You'd think she'd have learned." She put her hands on her hips. "Friedrich preferred me, too."

With a howl, Harriet sprang at Julia. Robbie caught her around the waist and held her back. "No. No."

"You can't care for her. She's trash. She should burn like the garbage she is."

Chief Bush was close at Robbie's shoulder. His voice was quiet, almost drowned by Harriet's howling. "Is that why you set the fires? To warn her?"

"Warn her. Oh yes." Harriet snarled. "She needs a warning to stop trying to take what doesn't belong to her." In a sudden passion she struggled to break free, but Robbie held tight. "She should burn. She deserves to burn. Of course, I set the fires, and I'd set a dozen more. I'd stone her. That's what I should have done first. I wish my brick had hit her instead of the car."

Chief Bush sounded regretful as he took her arm. "Miss Vines, there's no sense in getting riled up. It's time you and I go and have a talk with your parents."

"My parents?" Her voice shifted, becoming more docile. "Why would you wish to talk to my parents?"

"I think we need to tell them about some of the, uh, difficulties you're having. That would be nice, wouldn't it?" Bush's voice remained soothing like he was coaxing a toddler.

"I suppose they're better than talking to her." She brightened. "Do you think they'll be able to get her father's shop shut down? She knocked me down, you know. It would serve her right." Harriet remained focused on her grievance. "You're not going to bring her too, are you?"

"No." He looked at Julia over his shoulder. "Miss Wren, you're not allowed to come."

"We're going into the Park, and you're not allowed. That's the way it's supposed to be." Harriet was calm now. Back to her air of superiority. She brushed gloved fingers over her ruined dress, vainly trying to get rid of the stains.

Julia gave a halfhearted stomp of her foot, as she followed the chief's lead. "That's not fair."

"Well, too bad. Robbie never should have invited your kind into the Park at all. But I forgive you." She clasped Robbie's arm as the chief led her away, her fingers lingering longingly. "I forgive you, Robbie. I know it wasn't your fault. I know she's a temptress." Harriet continued expounding on her theory as the chief led her to his car and helped her in.

He turned back only briefly. "I'll talk to you two tomorrow."

Chapter 16

Now that it was over, Julia was so tired and shaky she considered curling up beneath the nearest tree and going to sleep. Only her consciousness of how chilly the night air had grown, and how damp the ground was likely to be kept her upright. As the chief drove off, she turned to trudge back to the ice cream parlor.

The ice cream parlor! It could have completely gone up in flames. A bolt of energy fired through her and she began to run.

Robbie jogged beside her. "What's wrong?"

"The fire. I don't know if there will be anything left." She groaned. "What was I thinking? Pop. He's going to be crushed."

"I took care of it."

"What?"

"I put it out. I knew those grenades would come in handy."

"You…" Julia slowed. "You put it out? Thank you." She grasped his hand and squeezed it, then released it just as quickly. "I don't know how to thank you."

Robbie brushed this aside. "I *am* learning how to function in the real world. I figured it was just another lesson." He gave her a sideways glance. "Believe me, knowing you has been an education."

Julia cut her eyes at him. "What's that supposed to mean?"

"Only good things."

She snorted. "I will overlook that because you saved the ice cream parlor."

They shared a grin and then fell quiet. Robbie offered her his arm. It was peaceful walking together. No obligation to keep the conversational ball in play. No expectations. Just quiet companionship.

She was going to miss him. She could admit that much to herself. It was going to be hard to return to school. But it would be harder to stay in Tuxedo Park and be unable to see him.

She sighed. Why did he have to be so charming? She stole a glance at his profile. And handsome?

He caught her glance and looked down at her. "Are you all right?"

And kind?

Her eyes filled.

He drew her close and she let her head rest against the hollow of his shoulder. His arms were warm and heavy around her shoulders. He stroked her hair with one hand. Best of all he gave her the gift of not demanding an explanation for her tears.

He was perfect. And she was sunk. She would never be a Parkie. Never be the society wife he needed to be successful in his world. There was no hope of a future for them unless she were to compromise herself. And she wouldn't.

Her throat burned and with an effort of will that tore her heart in two, she pulled free of his comforting arms. "Please don't bother to pick me up tomorrow. I'll walk." Turning, she pulled her spare hanky from her sleeve and dabbed at her eyes.

"Wait."

She stopped but, spine rigid, refused to turn back.

"Who will play Ariel?"

Relieved, she did swivel to face him. "I can. I know the part and the cues."

"All right." He gave a single nod. "I'll see you tomorrow."

She hurried off, only looking back when she had reached the ice cream parlor. He was still standing where she'd left him. Watching to make sure she arrived safely.

Julia arrived at the appointed time for the play with every muscle aching. She had scratches on her arms and one on her face from Harriet's talons, but she figured it would be covered by the stage makeup. She just wanted to get through the evening so that she could go home and lick her wounds. Next week she'd be back at school where she would be so busy she wouldn't have to think about Robbie. She sought refuge in the flower-bedecked, gold-trimmed ladies' lounge where the air smelled of rose water and the carpet was so thick her heels became lost in the plush. She changed into Ariel's costume and took a seat before one of the mirrors to apply her stage makeup.

Geraldine appeared at her shoulder. "That's Harriet's costume."

Weariness dulled Julia's flash of anger. "Harriet won't be coming tonight."

Chief Bush had come by to take Julia's statement that morning and he had shared that Harriet's parents had agreed to pay for the shed to be repaired, and to make restitution to her father and Robbie for the property damage Harriet had caused. Meanwhile, Harriet was being sent away for a rest cure. It didn't seem enough. But no one had been seriously hurt, so she reckoned it was as much as she could reasonably expect. Julia fervently hoped part of Harriet's treatment would include a kick in the pants from someone who could teach her that she wasn't the center of the universe.

"What do you mean she won't be here?" Geraldine's voice was sharp. "She wouldn't miss the play."

Julia shrugged in somewhat unladylike fashion. "That's what I heard. Perhaps you should ask her parents if they are here."

Geraldine narrowed her eyes, suspicious that something wasn't right. But Julia was in no mood to satisfy her curiosity. She turned back to the mirror and slathered on a layer of greasepaint.

As show time approached, Julia's malaise dissipated. Unbidden, excitement began to build in her chest, as she absorbed the jitters and flushed anticipation of the other cast members. It was her play after all. She wondered if she could get Professor Flitch to give her extra credit for not just writing it, but seeing it produced.

A seemingly endless stream of cast members presented themselves to her with concerns ranging from a ripped hem to an unfortunate boil that needed covering.

By the time the curtain went up, she had managed to shake off the last remnant of her mulligrubs. After all, she could relax now that the real arsonist had been caught.

As they waited for the curtain to go up, she joined the rest of the cast in stealing a peek at the audience. She didn't have any family members in the crowd. So she only had eyes for Robbie. Clad in a tuxedo he sat in the front row where he could prompt people with their lines if they became stuck.

He looked—she really didn't have a word for it. Could a man be beautiful, while not at all feminine? Whatever the word she was searching for, her stomach did a flip. And her heart seemed to expand and go all mushy around the edges. He caught her peeking and gave her a wink and a broad smile.

It felt like her insides were coated by warm butterscotch syrup. Sort of sweet and gooey.

Then her cue came and she strode out on stage, her heart as light as it had been all summer.

A Tempest in a Teapot proved to be more of a success than she might have expected when played before the very titans of industry it lampooned. The Parkies even laughed at the jokes.

At the end, Julia took a bow with the players.

Robbie seemed to be in his element as he bounded onto the stage. "Ladies and gentlemen, I know you will be as thrilled as I am to know that the talented author of tonight's entertainment is among us." He made a sweeping gesture toward Julia. "Miss Julia Wren."

Julia stood frozen, her expression fixed, as applause rippled through the room and her cheeks burned. Charlie nudged her forward and she scooted out of line by about six inches.

"Miss Wren is a local, and as I'm sure you all noted, very talented writer. We of the Park will all follow her career with great interest."

After thanks to the club for supporting the play, and all the actors, it was all over and Julia filed off stage with the others.

A thrill of accomplishment made her smile uncontrollably. It was done. They had done it. She and Robbie together. And despite the problems along the way, it had been done well.

A reception was scheduled to follow the play. Robbie had invited her, but Julia did not plan to attend. She had nothing suitable to wear. At least not when compared to Park standards. She knew very well how her pretty party dress would look when compared to the Worth evening gowns and gems worn by the Parkies. She dressed in the modest, pale blue dress with its lace and silver trim and examined herself in the looking glass. Would she trade what she had, her father, the ice cream parlor, her friends, her education, if it meant she could belong here?

What would it even be like to have everything one ever wanted? To never have to wash a sink full of dirty dishes. For that matter, never to have to cook a meal in the first place. To have food appear, to eat her fill and then have the leftovers spirited away sounded like the stuff of dreams.

The leisure wealth brought with it certainly had its appeal. But having met these girls now, she knew they were no happier or healthier than her friends. If anything they seemed less content. She caught sight of Geraldine's scowl as her maid handed her a gorgeous pale green silk gown dotted with seed pearls. Julia grinned and, unseen, saluted her image in the glass.

Nope. It was official. She was happy to be a Townie.

She found Gwen Banks and gave her a fond hug, then slipped out a side entrance.

The air outside was silky with the edge of rain that would arrive in a few hours. She strolled down the path, and away from the clubhouse for the last time. And she found that the thought wasn't so very troubling. The only thing she would truly miss about the Park was Robbie.

"Julia!"

It was as if her thoughts had conjured him. She stopped and turned. Flanking Robbie was her father looking as dapper as she had ever seen him in a black tuxedo, and on his other side, Professor Flitch in a gown of mulberry satin.

She blinked. "Pop?"

He beamed at her. "Mr. Malcolm invited us to attend. That play was something else. I'm proud of you, Julie Bean."

Professor Flitch nodded. "Count me genuinely impressed as well, Miss Wren. That was delightful."

Julia's neck and cheeks tingled with heat. "Thank you." She drew close enough for her father to pull her into a bear hug. "And thank you." She smiled at Robbie, trying to convey her sense of gratitude. There was no way they would have been allowed to attend the play at the clubhouse without an invitation from a member, and she knew perfectly well which member would have done that for her.

He grinned his charming rascal's grin and extended

his hand for a prim shake. Even knowing she shouldn't, she would have preferred an embrace. But she took the proffered hand, an electric zip shooting up her arm as she did so. How could the connection between them be so strong on so brief an acquaintance?

Heart pounding in her ears, she barely heard Pop inviting Robbie and Professor Flitch back to the ice cream parlor for a treat.

Robbie thanked him with every evidence of genuine pleasure. "Sir, would you mind if I borrow Julia for a moment? There are members of the audience and cast who would like to greet her."

Pop was expansive. "By all means. By all means. Bring them along, too. This is a night to celebrate. I'll go on ahead and get things ready."

"If it's all right, I would be happy to help you," Professor Flitch said.

Pop nodded. "I believe I'd like that."

Professor Flitch nodded a graceful farewell and allowed Pop to take her arm as they strolled down the drive. Julia could hear him talking about his talented daughter's bright future.

Julia shook her head. "Thank you again. I never dreamed that he would be able to be here tonight."

Robbie looked back at her with a gaze of such intensity that she knew she could not escape the conversation they were about to have. She'd just have to pray for God's help through it.

Robbie felt like there was a weight on his chest and if he waited a moment more he was going to explode. "I spoke to my father today."

She looked a little surprised at that, and he wondered fleetingly what she had expected him to say.

"It was not a pleasant chat."

"Did you tell him about your photography?"

"I did. I laid it out for him. He always admired his grandfather for making his own way and becoming a success. I explained that I wanted to do the same thing. And that I didn't want his money."

"Was he angry?"

Robbie nodded. "Indubitably. But without the threat of withholding money, he really doesn't have anything he can do about it, so he actually had to talk to me."

"Were you able to come to terms?"

He loved that she was able to ask the most pertinent question. "I think so." He smiled ruefully and rubbed his jaw. "I'm not going to get a dime from him as long as he lives. But, he may leave his wealth to my children if my marriage pleases him."

"That doesn't seem much of a compromise."

Robbie laughed. "For him it is. We will remain on speaking terms and if I fail, I can admit the folly of my ways and come home."

"So what are your plans?"

"I have a bequest from my grandmother. It's not a huge amount. Not when compared to my father's fortune, but it will be enough to get me started. I'm moving to New York and I'm going to start taking pictures and trying to sell them to the newspapers."

"Then you will freelance." She was animated. "If you get something really striking, instead of selling to the first paper willing to buy it, you could have them bid."

The little thrill of potential skittered up the back of

his neck. He loved her. There was no doubt about it. Who else would help him build his dreams and make them bigger, rather than trying to make him be "reasonable." "Right. And I could even do more if I could get in on some of the feature pieces."

"What do you mean?" She tilted her head.

"Well if I'm not tied to a particular paper, I won't necessarily know what they need for features. I suppose once I get established I might get some commissions. But I think it would be a good idea to partner with a freelance writer. We would both benefit by being able to present a whole package to the paper."

"Oh, yes. That would be a great idea."

"I'd like it to be you, Julia."

"Me?" Her eyes met his. Direct and questioning.

"I already know you can write. And I know you can sniff out nefarious doings. And you're going to be in New York."

Her eyes were sparkling and her cheeks flushed. "Do you really think I could do it?"

"I have no doubt. That is, if you want to." He paused and reached for her hand. "There's just one thing."

The sparkle in her eyes faded, and became something softer, more luminescent.

Throat dry as newsprint, he carried on. "You've inspired me. I never would have had the courage to consider a life outside the Park. Aside from that, you're the most fascinating woman I've ever met. I can't get you out of my mind, and I don't really want to."

"Robbie, you know it wouldn't work. Your father wouldn't approve of a match to someone like me."

"He's not marrying you."

She raised an eyebrow.

Robbie amended his answer. "I think it only fair that you know the plan." He wasn't sure if she would believe him, but he really had thought the matter all the way through. "He won't be happy with any young lady unless he chooses her for me. But I believe he will come to accept you. He is confidently expecting me to come crawling back to him on bended knee. And while he would get some satisfaction from that, I think he'd really be more pleased and proud if I did make a success of myself. My wife will need to be strong to withstand him and Mother, too. But they're not evil. They will come around. Especially if it means being able to see their grandchildren."

Her lips flattened as she tried to repress a smile.

Emboldened, he carried on. "So will you marry me? I already obtained your father's permission. I think he's at least as skeptical of me as my parents are of you."

She remained silent for a long minute and he started to grow nervous. Had he miscalculated? Had his father been right? He had to make sure she understood what she was getting. "I won't be able to offer you the life of a Park grandee."

She squeezed his hand. "Then the answer is yes. I never wanted to be a Parkie. I only want to be yours. And she all but tackled him in an enthusiastic embrace. Their lips joined, hers soft and sweet and he couldn't help but reach up to cup the back of her head. Her hair was silky smooth. The bones of her jaw, delicate and finely wrought like porcelain, though he knew she was made of sterner stuff.

The sort of stuff a man could build a future with.

Could really partner with to create a family and a life. They would not be one of those couples who tolerated one another so ill they lived an hour apart and saw one another only on the weekends. No. They would have a shared life. And he couldn't wait to get started.

* * * * *

REQUEST YOUR FREE BOOKS!

2 FREE INSPIRATIONAL NOVELS
PLUS 2
FREE
MYSTERY GIFTS

Love Inspired

YES! Please send me 2 FREE Love Inspired® novels and my 2 FREE mystery gifts (gifts are worth about $10). After receiving them, if I don't wish to receive any more books, I can return the shipping statement marked "cancel." If I don't cancel, I will receive 6 brand-new novels every month and be billed just $4.74 per book in the U.S. or $5.24 per book in Canada. That's a savings of at least 21% off the cover price. It's quite a bargain! Shipping and handling is just 50¢ per book in the U.S. and 75¢ per book in Canada.* I understand that accepting the 2 free books and gifts places me under no obligation to buy anything. I can always return a shipment and cancel at any time. Even if I never buy another book, the two free books and gifts are mine to keep forever.

105/305 IDN F49N

Name _____ (PLEASE PRINT) _____

Address _____ Apt. # _____

City _____ State/Prov. _____ Zip/Postal Code _____

Signature (if under 18, a parent or guardian must sign)

Mail to the Harlequin® Reader Service:
IN U.S.A.: P.O. Box 1867, Buffalo, NY 14240-1867
IN CANADA: P.O. Box 609, Fort Erie, Ontario L2A 5X3

**Are you a subscriber to Love Inspired books
and want to receive the larger-print edition?
Call 1-800-873-8635 or visit www.ReaderService.com.**

* Terms and prices subject to change without notice. Prices do not include applicable taxes. Sales tax applicable in N.Y. Canadian residents will be charged applicable taxes. Offer not valid in Quebec. This offer is limited to one order per household. Not valid for current subscribers to Love Inspired books. All orders subject to credit approval. Credit or debit balances in a customer's account(s) may be offset by any other outstanding balance owed by or to the customer. Please allow 4 to 6 weeks for delivery. Offer available while quantities last.

Your Privacy—The Harlequin® Reader Service is committed to protecting your privacy. Our Privacy Policy is available online at www.ReaderService.com or upon request from the Harlequin Reader Service.
We make a portion of our mailing list available to reputable third parties that offer products we believe may interest you. If you prefer that we not exchange your name with third parties, or if you wish to clarify or modify your communication preferences, please visit us at www.ReaderService.com/consumerschoice or write to us at Harlequin Reader Service Preference Service, P.O. Box 9062, Buffalo, NY 14269. Include your complete name and address.

LIDIR13R

REQUEST YOUR FREE BOOKS!

2 FREE INSPIRATIONAL NOVELS
PLUS 2
FREE
MYSTERY GIFTS

Love Inspired
HISTORICAL
INSPIRATIONAL HISTORICAL ROMANCE

YES! Please send me 2 FREE Love Inspired® Historical novels and my 2 FREE mystery gifts (gifts are worth about $10). After receiving them, if I don't wish to receive any more books, I can return the shipping statement marked "cancel." If I don't cancel, I will receive 4 brand-new novels every month and be billed just $4.74 per book in the U.S. or $5.24 per book in Canada. That's a savings of at least 21% off the cover price. It's quite a bargain! Shipping and handling is just 50¢ per book in the U.S. and 75¢ per book in Canada.* I understand that accepting the 2 free books and gifts places me under no obligation to buy anything. I can always return a shipment and cancel at any time. Even if I never buy another book, the two free books and gifts are mine to keep forever.

102/302 IDN F5CY

Name	(PLEASE PRINT)	
Address		Apt. #
City	State/Prov.	Zip/Postal Code

Signature (if under 18, a parent or guardian must sign)

Mail to the **Harlequin® Reader Service:**
IN U.S.A.: P.O. Box 1867, Buffalo, NY 14240-1867
IN CANADA: P.O. Box 609, Fort Erie, Ontario L2A 5X3

Want to try two free books from another series?
Call 1-800-873-8635 or visit www.ReaderService.com.

* Terms and prices subject to change without notice. Prices do not include applicable taxes. Sales tax applicable in N.Y. Canadian residents will be charged applicable taxes. Offer not valid in Quebec. This offer is limited to one order per household. Not valid for current subscribers to Love Inspired Historical books. All orders subject to credit approval. Credit or debit balances in a customer's account(s) may be offset by any other outstanding balance owed by or to the customer. Please allow 4 to 6 weeks for delivery. Offer available while quantities last.

Your Privacy—The Harlequin® Reader Service is committed to protecting your privacy. Our Privacy Policy is available online at www.ReaderService.com or upon request from the Harlequin Reader Service.

We make a portion of our mailing list available to reputable third parties that offer products we believe may interest you. If you prefer that we not exchange your name with third parties, or if you wish to clarify or modify your communication preferences, please visit us at www.ReaderService.com/consumerschoice or write to us at Harlequin Reader Service Preference Service, P.O. Box 9062, Buffalo, NY 14269. Include your complete name and address.

LIHDIR13R

April 15, 16, 2016

ReaderService.com

Manage your account online!

- Review your order history
- Manage your payments
- Update your address

*We've designed
the Harlequin® Reader Service
website just for you.*

Enjoy all the features!

- Reader excerpts from any series
- Respond to mailings and
  special monthly offers
- Discover new series available to you
- Browse the Bonus Bucks catalog
- Share your feedback

Visit us at:
ReaderService.com

RS13